ZOLI'S LEGACY

BOOK I: INHERITANCE

DAWN L. WATKINS

Library of Congress Cataloging-in-Publication Data:

Watkins, Dawn L.
  Zoli's legacy / Dawn L. Watkins.

     Contents: bk. 1. Inheritance—bk. 2. Bequest
     Summary: Zoli, a student in Hungary between the world wars, struggles for his education against poverty, his father's displeasure, and his own pride. As Hungary is drawn into the conflict of World War II, Zoli takes charge of an orphanage, marries, and becomes a soldier and father.
     ISBN 0-89084-596-4 (v. 1)—ISBN 0-89084-597-2 (v. 2)
     1. Hungary—History—1918-1945—Juvenile fiction.   [1. Hungary—History—1918-1945—Fiction.   2. Christian life—Fiction.]
I. Title.
PZ7.W268Zo   1991
[Fic]—dc20   91-29300
                                                              CIP
                                                              AC

Zoli's Legacy
Book I: Inheritance

Dawn L. Watkins

Edited by Carolyn Cooper and Rebecca S. Moore

©1991 Bob Jones University Press
Greenville, South Carolina 29614

ISBN 0-89084-596-4

20   19   18   17   16   15   14   13   12   11   10   9   8   7

Acknowledgments
Special thanks to Peter Gaal for interviews and tapes,
and to Lisa Gaal and Molly Bulla
for careful and patient transcription.

CZECHO-
LOVAKIA

■ Hungary today
□ Part of Hungary before
   the Treaty of Trianon

RUMANIA

Publisher's Note

The two volumes of *Zoli's Legacy* follow Zoltán Galambos through thirty years of Hungarian history, marking his choices and revealing their outcomes. Although the times around him are unsettled–from World War I until just after World War II–Zoli has a legacy that sustains him and that throughout proves larger than any circumstances.

Book I: Inheritance opens at the close of World War I in Hungary. Nicholas Horthy, a former Austro-Hungarian admiral, had organized a Hungarian army from what troops were left and had ridden into Budapest to restore order in the capital. Some viewed his action as heroic; some viewed it as the hopeless gesture of the eccentric. The Treaty of Trianon, part of the Peace of Versailles, had dismembered Hungary, putting parts under Czech, Rumanian, Austrian, and Serbian rule. But the Magyar people rallied with their traditional spirit against being assimilated into the new cultures.

The second part of the story takes place during the Horthy years, the admiral having been selected regent by the parliament and managing to stem the threat of Marxism to his country. Devastated by the war and penalized with huge war reparations, Hungary seemed about to sink into economic ruin. Horthy's government applied for membership in the League of Nations and instituted domestic programs. The displaced citizens of Hungary and the Hungarians still in the much-reduced homeland all believed that Hungary would someday regain its territories.

In this volume, Zoli Galambos comes not only to understand his national heritage but also to discover that there are other, more immediate legacies laid before him–his father's traditions, his mother's inheritance, his teacher's message of eternal life. His sharp mind and his constant observations draw him toward his choice. His brother Victor at the same time is eyeing his own choices. The choices that Zoli and Victor make early in their lives establish paths that diverge and have far different outcomes.

Contents

Part I: **Listen for the Train**

Part II: **Nobody's Boy**

Part I

LISTEN FOR THE TRAIN

1919-1930

*Mark the perfect man, and behold the upright:
for the end of that man is peace.*

Psalm 37:37

Chapter One
The White Horse

1919

If someone were to ask me the first thing I remember, I could tell him. If he asked me why I remember it, I could not say. I have heard that you remember a thing early if it awakes some emotion in you, and perhaps that is often so. I think I remember what I do because it was important to the adults. But maybe it was just that I liked horses.

It was morning. My father's breath went out in little white puffs before his lips. Hard snow crunched under his boots. And the wide wool of his collar rubbed my cheek as he ran with me in his arm.

I wanted to walk, but I was afraid to say so. I had never been in a city before; there were so many people and stone buildings and horses. I could hear the horses snorting and the snow crunching under the men's boots, but I did not hear the people talking.

My father ran up the steps of one of the gray buildings and turned around. There was a river–it was the Danube, but I did not know it then–and a long bridge. I looked a little sideways at my father. He did not look at me; he looked at the bridge.

After a long time, then, out of the frost on the other side, there came a great white horse, a gleaming, bobbing white horse. The man who rode it wore a long coat that spread out on either side of the saddle. He wore shiny black boots, his heels so low that his feet and legs made a V.

Behind the horse came rows and rows of soldiers. *Trump, trump, trump,* they marched, as steady as a heartbeat. On our side, everyone was looking toward the horse, not moving or talking. My father's arm stiffened against my legs. His chest moved in and out faster.

When the white horse stepped off the bridge on our side of the river, a man near us shouted something and threw his cap into the air. Then another man did the same. And suddenly everyone was running and shouting. But my father just stood on the stone steps, looking.

The white horse went by us, the leather on it shining. The rider did not look at us or wave. The bill of his hat almost covered his eyes. Papa's belt buckle hurt my knee.

''Who, Papa?'' I said.

''Nobody,'' said my father. ''Nobody.''

''That's Admiral Horthy, boy,'' said a man on our steps. ''Remember the day you saw Horthy ride his white horse over the Red Star of Marx.''

My father did not say anything. I could still see the white horse and the rider with the big coat. I could not see the red star they walked over. But I thought they looked handsome. I thought they looked like Hungary.

1920

''Zoltán!''

My father's voice jerked me awake.

"Coming, Papa!"

I pulled on my clothes and came into the kitchen.

"Lazy," he said. He ate his bread and cheese without turning to see me. "Do your chores–you have work here, you know. Life is not all school and playing."

"Yes, Papa. I'm sorry."

My brother Victor was crying. Mama handed him to me because he needed to be changed.

"Don't begrudge the boy his school," I heard Mama say to Papa. "He is my son too."

"What of that?" said Papa.

"You forget, do you!" Mama said. "I am the daughter of the mayor. I brought more inheritance to this house than you."

She rapped the wooden spoon against the pot more than she had to to clean the spoon.

Papa stood up so suddenly his chair fell backwards.

"The chores," he said to me and went out.

I put Victor in the cradle and ran to get my cap. Mama grabbed my arm at the door. She had such eyes, such eyes to look into you.

"You can be somebody, Zoltán. School will make you something." She stared into me until I trembled and looked down.

She let me go, and I escaped to the barn. The smell of hay and cows closed over me, and the safety of the early shadows. In the dimness, my father was swearing to himself as he milked.

Quietly I raked the stalls and put down new straw. I poured grain into the boxes for the horses, pouring it slowly, to watch the pile peak up and the grains roll down the sides. I fed the cows, careful to stay behind Papa's milking.

I went out the back door and looked toward the house. I could see the lamp burning low in the kitchen until Mama passed by the window and blocked it.

Then I picked some cherries from my grandfather's trees for my breakfast. My father's father did not speak to us, although he lived next door. But I felt he liked me and would want me to have the cherries, so long as I did not cause trouble by asking for them or did not get caught like a thief taking them.

I was at school too early–again. I was in the first year and so had nothing to do there early, but I went anyway and sat in whatever seat I wanted and pretended to read the books until the door handle turned with its little warning squeak.

The teacher came in a little while, banging his boots against the steps outside.

"Zoltán," he said. "Early again, eh?"

I nodded.

He hung up his hat on the peg by the door. He looked at me as if he might ask me something. But instead he went to his locked book cupboard and took out a huge book.

"Tell you what. When you come early, I want you to sing. Like the others who come early sometimes. Do you know any songs?"

"No, sir."

"Not one?"

I shook my head.

"Well, then, I'll teach you some."

The cover of the book said *Zsoltáros Könyv* in gold letters.

"These," he said, "are the Psalms set to music."

What were the Psalms, I wondered. He opened the book and chose a song. He sang it to me, but I did not especially like it.

Across the page were some words in lines that went in and out on one side, like a torn paper.

"What's this one say?" I said.

He lifted the book to see the page better.

"Ah," he said, "that one is for sadder hearts than yours."

* * *

"Don't sing in the barn," Papa said. "You are spoiling the air with your goose sounds."

I stopped singing, suddenly aware that I had been.

"And tomorrow," said Papa, "you tell the teacher that school is out for you. I want you here. What does a man have a son for if not to work for him?"

"Yes, Papa," I said. But I was afraid to think of telling the teacher I was leaving three weeks before school was out.

That day I was not early to school. The village was still, no one in the stores, no women calling out to each other. Only the swineherd was out, prodding the pigs with his stick. I thought it was because I was so much later than usual that things in my village of Szilas were so quiet. At school the teacher had not yet come, but somehow we felt we should not sing.

When at last the teacher came, he stood for a long moment in the doorway, looking at us. Then he walked to the front of the room and signed the class book as he did every day. But he did not call for us to stand and recite. He just stood looking down, as though he were seeing the saddest sight in the world, as though the rough boards under his feet were full of awful words.

Then the bells of the church began to chime. They rang and rang and rang, but not with any tune, just a jumbled clanging. We looked at each other and back to the teacher. He was bringing out a map of Hungary, and without a word, he held it up to us. We all looked at the map and at our teacher until, at last, the bells stopped ringing and there was silence, like snow, everywhere.

"Our country, our empire which has stood a thousand years," the teacher said, "has survived the Great War. But now–" and here his voice shook and his eyes were suddenly full of tears, "but now I do not think we can survive the peace."

He held the map against the plank wall and cut it into five pieces with a knife. One by one the pieces fell to the floor, and he made no move to stop them.

"The Treaty of Trianon," he said, "has cut us into bits. We are no longer Hungarians."

Even in my father's house I had never heard such a silence.

"Who are we then?" a boy asked at last.

"We are," the teacher said with a strange tone in his voice, "Czechoslovakians."

"Just like that?" the boy asked, for all of us.

The teacher nodded.

"How?" said the boy.

"The treaty has ripped up our empire and given part of us to Yugoslavia, and part to Rumania, and part to Aust–" The teacher broke off, and his jaw muscles worked.

"Who is the king?" asked another.

"There is no king. Charles IV was the last king of Hungary. Remember that, those of you who can."

The teacher straightened his shoulders.

"We have a Regent now," he told us. "Admiral Horthy. A Hungarian admiral."

I rarely spoke in school. So I do not know if it was what I said that surprised the teacher–or that I had said anything at all.

"Will he ride his white horse over the red star again?"

"God help us," he said. "I hope so."

The bells began to toll again. The teacher put his hand to his eyes.

I thought of the white horse and wondered what would become of us all.

Chapter Two
No, No, Never

1923

"Look, Papa," I said after supper. "I have something to show you."

I held out a paper to him. My heart pounded so that I thought he might hear it. I watched his mouth, the corners of it. He stared at the paper without taking it.

"It's all *excellents*," I said. "I have top marks in everything, Papa."

His mustache hung down limp on each side of his face.

"That's your job, to do it well."

Still I stood there.

"Well," he said, "what do you want?"

I stepped back, but I held the paper in front of me.

"I was the best third-year student," I whispered.

Mama took the paper.

"There is hope for you," she said.

She smoothed the paper out on top of the book she was reading and looked at it.

"You could be a pastor," she said.

I felt my surprise. It surged through me, like extra blood.

Papa snorted. "A pastor? What for?"

"Because," Mama said, "the pastor makes the most money and has the easiest job. He has a bathtub in his house."

"You talk like a woman," said Papa.

Mama stood up and lifted her chin.

"And you can talk only like a stupid farmer."

Papa looked up and in a low, low voice, like water nearly ready to boil, said, "Never speak to me like that again, or I shall answer it." His eyes burned at her. "Do you hear? Never."

Mama stood there, looking like ice, and did not open her mouth. She never said anything like it again, but the idea lived on in the house just the same.

1924

The cherry trees drooped with the cherries hanging on them. Dots of red and pink wavered among the leaves when the wind blew.

"Victor," I said one morning, "want some cherries? I can get them for us."

"Oh, Zoli," he said, "we'll get caught."

"No, we won't," I said. "I know what to do. Come on."

He hung back.

"I used to get them all the time when I was little as you," I said.

Victor looked at the trees in Grandfather's back yard and then at me. I knew how much he wanted the cherries because there were never enough sweets for little boys in Szilas. Then he smiled.

Papa was in the fields, and Grandfather was in the village. I had checked that out.

"Stay here under the tree," I said, "and I'll drop them down to you."

He stood there with wide eyes, ready to run. He was not a coward, my brother; he was only five.

I ate the nicest red cherries from the top of the tree, and the pink half-ripe ones I let fall to the ground because I loved my brother but not quite as much as myself.

When my mouth was full and juice running out, I dropped some bright reds to Victor. He leaped for them and grabbed them up, as though I might change my mind and will them back up to the tree if he hesitated.

Then I saw Grandfather through the leaves. He was coming back from the village with his cane, limping on his bad leg.

I slid down to the next branch. I could see Victor picking up cherries and stuffing them into his mouth. I slid down to the next branch.

"Victor," I whispered, "Gran–"

With a snap the branch let go and I fell straight down, like a stone into a well. I hit my jaw square on Victor's head, and we dropped together into the grass without a sound. Everything turned gray, and I felt suddenly sick. I sat up in a daze.

Victor held the top of his head, and silent tears ran out of his eyes. I tried to reach for him, but I couldn't. Then he was pulling at me.

"Hurry, hurry."

I put my hand to my jaw. I felt no pain. I pushed, and there was a snap, a sudden sickening snap, like a mousetrap.

Victor ran along the fence onto our side of the line. I crawled behind him, trying not to be sick, trying to be quiet.

At supper that evening I couldn't open my jaws.

"Why don't you want your sausage?" Mama asked.

I shook my head.

She took the sausage and gave it to Victor.

"More milk, please?" I asked. I tried not to move my jaw.

She gave me another cup of milk and did not notice how I drank it, from the side of my mouth, or that my eyes watered when I swallowed.

That night as we lay on our pallet, Victor studied my face in the moonlight.

"This side is bigger," he said, and reached toward my cheek.

I stopped his hand.

"Don't tell Mama," I said through my teeth, "or I will say how many cherries you had."

"I won't."

He lay back and was quiet. Then he raised up on his elbow and looked at me again.

"Why doesn't Grandfather want us to have his cherries?"

"I don't know. Go to sleep."

* * *

"From now on," said Papa, "you will help with the milking. Here is a pail. Start down there."

It was dim in the stalls, but not dark enough for lanterns. The cattle chewed and snorted. I took the pail, its handle cold in my hand.

"How do I do it, Papa?"

Papa looked down at me, not angry exactly. He looked as though he hadn't slept in a long time.

"How can I have a son so stupid?" he said. "Already you have seen it so many times. You are supposed to learn by looking."

He walked away and set to his own milking. I tried to watch from a distance, but his hands moved so fast that I could hardly tell what he did. His fingers squeezed and rolled in one long movement. Squeeze and roll, squeeze and roll, and milk streamed out into the pail.

My father shifted his position, and I leaned back into the shadows. I tried to look again but his hands were too far under the cow. I went to the other end of the barn, to the oldest cow.

I set down the pail and tried to imitate my father's motions. But no milk came. I pulled harder. The cow stamped her foot and swung her head toward me. Behind me Papa's pail rattled, and I knew he was standing up, that he might be coming.

My fingers were cold, and my hands shook. "Please," I said, my jaw aching from the clenching. "Please," I said again into the growing darkness.

I squeezed and rolled my thumb and finger together again. Milk spurted into the pail so suddenly that I jumped. Again and again I copied the motions. Again and again the milk squirted into the pail.

When I realized that I was holding my breath, I leaned back and sucked in a mouthful of air. I saw then that Victor was beside me, watching silently.

I milked three cows before Papa caught up to me. I might have smiled, but the pain was still too much.

I held the pail out to Papa.

Papa took my pail and looked into it. He said nothing, but he almost smiled, I think.

Victor watched Papa walk away. And when he looked back, his eyes looked much older to me.

*   *   *

"No, no, never!"

It was a chant, coming from the school.

"No, no, never!"

The early comers crouched in a knot at the front, shouting the words and banging their fists in rhythm.

"No, no, never!"

"Zoli," said one of the boys. "Come on."

"Are we Czechs?" called a boy.

"No, no, never!" we replied.

When the teacher came, we disbanded and took our seats.

"So," he said to us, "you have a new song, do you?"

I looked down, knowing the preservation of silence.

"So shall we all," he said. "Stand up."

We raised our heads and stood up slowly.

"Repeat this," said the teacher. "I believe in one God."

"I believe in one God."

"I believe in one country."

"I believe in one country."

"I believe in a holy and eternal truth."

"I believe in a holy and eternal truth."

"I believe in the resurrection of Hungary!"

"I believe in the resurrection of Hungary!"

My jaw hurt so that when I said the words my eyes watered. The teacher came and put his hand on my shoulder.

"The day will come, Zoltán," he said.

I did not say that it was my jaw that brought the tears.

"Czechoslovakia," he said to us all, "is a made-up word. We are not Czechs; we are not Slovaks."

"*Nem, nem, soha!*" we said. "No, no, never!"

My father was always in his newspapers. Mostly he read the crop prices. But if Horthy's picture appeared, he read that paper over and over.

At supper Papa said, "In school do they teach you *nem, nem, soha*?"

"Yes, sir." *Papa* was too hard to say.

He nodded.

Mama said, "We have some cherries tonight from the market. Here, Victor. Zoltán?"

"Just milk, please," I said. But I was thinking, *No, no, never again cherries.*

Chapter Three
The Ticket Out

1925

"Your jaw sticks out," said Victor. He leaned on his pitchfork to study my face. "Your bottom teeth are ahead of the top ones."

He gathered a forkful of hay. "You look like Grandfather." He laughed and shook hay loose from the fork and into the chute.

"You finish," I said. "I have to start the milking."

"Teach me how to milk, Zoli. Won't you? What if Papa tells me to and I can't?"

I hesitated, one leg on the ladder, the other in the mow. I wanted to say that no one had taught me. But I didn't.

"Come down in a little, but don't let Papa see you."

He learned almost as quickly as I could show him.

"Roll down on your thumb. Like this."

Victor got milk the first time.

"That's good," I said.

He moved in, and I shuffled over some, to let him try with both hands. The old cow chewed slowly and blinked, but she never swung her head back toward us.

We rinsed the pails and hung them up. I walked toward the house through the orchard rather than taking the path, and Victor followed me a while and then went back to the path. When we got near the house, through the window we could hear the hard voices, always the hard voices.

"He *will*," said Mama. "Keep Victor home, but Zoltán will go to school. He is like my father–a cut above–"

"You will not tell me what to do with my sons!"

"On this I will!" My mother's voice had a wildness in it. "On this I will throw down all else!"

Victor did not look at me, or at anything. He turned back for the barn. I felt there was nowhere to go. Perhaps, I thought, if I stood still, I would become a cherry tree, useful and not troublesome, cared for without dislike, and tall enough to be above the angers of the house.

*   *   *

My brother Béla was born in the winter. He cried more than Victor had. Mama was too sick to stay up long at a time. So Victor and I changed Béla and carried him to Mama when she called.

In the evenings, I taught Victor what I had learned in school, bringing home books and stories to tell and rows of numbers I memorized from the lessons.

"I don't want to do this anymore," he said one night. He pushed away the pencil and the paper.

"Come on, Victor, you can spell this easy."

"I don't want to."

"Do you want to be a farmer forever?"

"Yes." Victor looked at me as if I were crazy. "Don't you?"

"No." I pushed back from the table and looked at him. Then, after some moments, I brought out my secret. "I am going to be a doctor."

Victor continued to stare at me.

"Look." I pulled up a book from a stack on the floor. "See this picture? This is a famous doctor named Albert Schweitzer. I'm going to Africa to help him."

"Africa?" Victor now looked at me as though he should pick up something to protect himself with. "Where is that?"

I leafed to a map. "Here. And here is where we are." Victor's astonishment gave way to curiosity. He bent over the map. "I bet you can't spell *Africa*," I said.

"Zoltán," my mother called. "Béla is crying. Bring him here."

"Béla," I whispered to Victor, "bosses us around."

As soon as I picked Béla up, he stopped crying and smiled. His face was still red from the work of running my life.

We stood by Mama's bed. The dirt floor was cold, even in the summers.

Victor said, "Zoli is going to Africa."

My mother looked up at him. "What do you mean?" She was not surprised; she was quick, my mother.

"To be a Schweitzer," said Victor.

My mother turned her gaze to me.

"I told him I was going to be a doctor," I said.

Mama leaned back into her pillow and smiled more than she had in as long as I could remember. "Victor," she said, "go get Béla his blanket."

When Victor left, Mama said, "I promise you will get all I inherited from my father when you become a doctor. My son Zoltán will be somebody."

This all she said more to herself than to me.

1929

The city judge came to our house one morning before breakfast. He wore his ribbon badge and his hat. He did not look like a judge to me. He looked like a shopkeeper who had won a prize.

"Your second boy is supposed to be in school," he said to Papa. "That is the law."

Papa said nothing. Dezső, my third brother, cried in his cradle, and my mother got up to tend him.

"The Gymnásium will be sending a professor here to the school to decide whether the boy should be put in the first year or in the third year according to his age." He attempted a smile.

My heart jumped. A professor from the Gymnásium, the high school in Komárom I would go to in the fall, if I could get the money.

Again Papa said nothing.

The judge waited, turning his hat in his hand. At last he looked at Victor. "Tomorrow, young man, be at the school." He put on the hat and adjusted it. "Good day, then."

When he was gone, Victor said, "What should I do, Papa?"

"What they say to, I suppose," said Papa.

In bed that night I said to my brother, "I'll go with you, Victor. Don't worry. You'll do fine. You know as much as I do, and I'm going to the Gymnásium."

A long while later–I was almost asleep–Victor said, "How will you go without money and with me at school? Who will help Papa?"

"We'll all help. You and me and Béla even. And I'll get the money somehow."

"You are a dreamer, Zoli. And no good can come of it. Papa says so."

Victor and I were at the school early. It was July; no one else would be coming. In an hour or so, the city judge came in. Behind him was a gray-haired man with small round spectacles. He had a bushy mustache and heavy gray eyebrows. But when he smiled, all I noticed were his blue eyes.

"This is the boy, sir," said the judge, pointing to Victor.

"And your name is?" the professor said to Victor.

"Victor Galambos, sir."

"Well, let's see where you are, Victor, shall we?"

He opened a book to a map of the world. I went to the back and sat down on the wooden bench under the window. I felt as though I might get sick.

"Can you show me where Czechoslovakia is?" the professor said.

"Here," said Victor. "But that's a made-up name, you know."

"Yes," said the professor, glancing at the judge, but smiling a little.

"And here is Africa," Victor went on.

The sun came in on me, just making a triangle on my shoulder at first. Then it spread across my neck and then onto my other shoulder. The professor's voice came and went around me, like a pleasant summer wind that gusts once in a while and makes you remember it is there.

Two hours later, the professor gathered up his books and maps and patted Victor's head.

"That's enough for me," he said. "We'll put you in the third year–but you could be fourth or fifth. Who's your teacher, son?"

Victor pointed back at me. "My brother teaches me his lessons at night."

"Well, well."

The man looked at me, and I felt somehow that he too could warm a person, like the sun, if he wanted to.

"Let me walk you boys home," the professor said.

Victor and I had no words to stop him, though I felt I should find some. He asked us about Szilas, about our farm. Victor, I thought, talked too much.

When we came to the house, I ran ahead to tell Papa.

Papa shook the man's hand, but he did not return the professor's smile.

"Mr. Galambos," the professor said, "I am Henrik Kovaly, from the Gymnásium in Komárom. I'm pleased to tell you that Victor is ready to enter school at the third year."

Papa did not look at Victor. "Fine."

"And," the professor said, "Zoltán here tells me he is fourteen. He could come to the Gymnásium next fall."

"There is no money for that," said Papa.

"Yes," said the man, "so it is for all Hungary now. But in the Gymnásium, for a few students who are especially able, there is work that can be done in exchange for schooling. Tutoring–teaching subjects to the slower students." He looked hopefully at Papa.

"He has work here."

"Isn't that mostly in the summer? Perhaps you would consid–"

"Zoltán has graduated from elementary school. It is enough."

My mother appeared in the doorway, looking out at us. But she said nothing.

"Well, as you say, of course," said Kovaly. "But I do hate to see the positions go to the Czechs when Hungary has so much to offer."

He shook my father's hand again, said good-bye to Victor and me, and walked back toward the train station. I felt as though my whole future was about to get on a train and leave Szilas forever. I did not know whether the brightness of that afternoon would be enough to last me all my life.

After the milking that evening, I hung my pail in its place. Papa came in behind me and began sloshing water around in his pail to clean it.

"Can you write a letter?" he asked.

"Yes, Papa."

He turned the bucket over, and the water splashed down.

"Then write Kovaly. Say that you will come to him in September—"

It seemed he would say more, but he stopped.

My head felt as though it might burst. My eyes stung. But I knew better than to show excitement or to ask what had changed.

"Yes, Papa," I said, as though he had said to me only "shut the door."

Papa hung up his pail and went out.

I climbed the loft ladder and went as high as I could into the hay. I imagined I could see the smoke from the train. I did not think that anything could be better than to get on a train to Komárom. But then I was a peasant in Szilas, and very young, and did not know what life might become.

Chapter Four
Black Shoe Polish

The clock struck–at last. I had been awake most of the night, waiting for my life to start. I dressed in the dark and went out to do the chores.

The pail was not on the peg. I looked in the barn for it, but it was nowhere. After a while, Papa came in, followed by Victor.

"Papa," I said, "my pail is gone. I–"

"Your pail? What do you need with a pail, schoolboy? You go off when you finally might be a little use to me. No, you don't need a pail."

Then I saw that Papa had both pails, one inside the other. He pulled them apart and handed one to Victor. My brother took the pail and walked past me to the other end of the barn. He didn't look at me, and I felt as though right there, in the barn, in the lantern light, I had lost what little I had in the world. I stood there, empty-handed and invisible, with the sounds of cows and milking around me in the damp. I put down hay just the same.

I walked the three miles to the train station and bought a ticket with money Professor Kovaly had sent. It was an hour's ride to Komárom, but the only thing I remember is how the fog lifted on the way.

The train station in Komárom was bigger and busier than the one in my village. It had a long platform, and at one end a garden of flowers shaped like a map of Hungary. It was an old map, as Hungary was before the treaty. I wondered how it was that the Czechs, who now owned Komárom, let it stay there.

*   *   *

"Excuse me," I said, "where do I go to register?"

The Gymnásium turned out to be a building shaped like a squared-off horseshoe, three stories high. The boy looked at me but did not answer. He wore a white shirt with a full collar. His smile turned up only one side of his lips.

"Where can I find Professor Kovaly?"

"What language are you speaking?" the boy said to me. His voice was low, and his Hungarian barely recognizable to me.

"Hungarian."

"What kind of Hungarian?" He laughed. "Where are you from?"

Two more boys, older than I, joined him.

"What's this?" said one.

The other leaned toward me and sniffed.

"Smells like a cow!"

The boys roared.

"Looks like a cow *yard,*" said the first fellow.

We all followed his gaze toward my feet. Mud was caked on my shoes and spattered on the legs of my pants. My face got hot, and I would have flung a comment back, but I was more embarrassed about my accent than my clothes.

A man appeared behind the boys. He was young and tall and serious. A gold chain hung between his vest button and his pocket.

"What's so funny, gentlemen?"

The boys lost their smiles.

"Nothing, sir," said one.

"Then be gone," he said, and they went.

I tried to make my dirty shoes inconspicuous, but my feet seemed at that moment as big as stumps.

"You're new, I take it?" he said.

"Yes, sir." I paused. "I am Zoltán Galambos."

"Well, Zoltán, the rules are that shoes are shined and clothes are neat."

"Yes, sir."

"Where do you live?"

"In Szilas."

"Ah. Are you a tutor?"

"Yes. First year. Professor Kovaly said to come to him–but I can't find him."

"Kovaly, is it? Come with me."

We went to a small room where the man unlocked a door. He motioned me inside. Trunks, chests, and wardrobes stood along all the walls and in the middle of the floor. The man opened a chest. It was filled with shoes.

"What size?" he asked.

"I–I don't know."

"Well, try on some until a pair fits and take them."

"But–I haven't any money yet."

"These things are for deserving students in need. You are in need. And I trust you will prove yourself deserving."

I found a pair that fit. The man handed me a pair of trousers.

"These should be all right. Now then, tomorrow I expect to see a proper Gymnásium student. Yes?"

"Yes, sir. Thank you, sir."

He nodded. And I determined to be worthy of the shoes–and the trust.

* * *

The Latin class met in a bright room with ten tall windows. I chose a seat by a window. The other half of the seat was empty, and I hoped it would remain so. The other boys talked and laughed. I just looked at my new shoes.

The door opened, and all the students stood up. A professor came in, pulling the door shut, and turned toward the class. It was Professor Kovaly.

He smiled at the lot of us.

"Be seated, gentlemen. Now then, to begin to learn, you must know Latin. We will begin by memorizing certain useful words. Repeat after me: *ante, apud, ad, adversum.*"

"*Ante, apud, ad, adversum.*"

"*Ad, adversum, circum, circa.*"

Sometime later, not so long it seemed, a boy passed by the door, ringing a bell.

"Dismissed," said Kovaly, "except–"

Twenty boys froze in various stages of exit.

"Mr. Galambos."

Nineteen boys, relieved, went on moving. I remained, frozen.

"Zoltán, I'm glad to see you. I want to take you to meet the young man you'll be tutoring this year. All right?"

"Yes, sir. Thank you. And thank you for the train money. I'll pay you back as soon as I can."

"I know you will. Now let's be going."

The student sat on a stone bench outside. He was blonde, handsome, well dressed. He did not stand as the professor approached.

"Pali," said Professor, "this is Zoltán. Zoltán, this is Pali, your student."

Pali took me in with a glance, toe to head. He did not offer his hand; so I did not offer mine.

Professor said to me, "Pali is a first-year Gymnásium student, like you. Only–"

Pali cocked his head, looking up sideways at us.

"Only this is his second first year," Kovaly finished. The teacher smiled his smile. "I think you can change Pali's record, Zoltán."

Pali crossed his ankle over his knee. He adjusted his position slightly. "Thank you, Professor."

"Good day, then, Pali," the teacher said. "Zoltán, a word more, if you please."

As we walked away, back toward the classroom building, he pulled a small tin from his pocket.

"I thought you could use this."

"What is it?"

"Shoe polish."

He walked on without waiting to be thanked.

At three o'clock I caught the train back to Szilas. At four I was jogging home to change clothes and do what chores were left me.

Next morning I washed and polished my shoes in the washroom of the train. The black leather shined. Another boy, from a different village, was in there scrubbing the mud from his socks and trouser legs.

"Say," he said, "could I use a little polish?"

His country accent comforted me. I held out the tin, though his shoes, I saw, were brown. He took a tiny dab on his finger. Then he smeared the polish on his left heel and pulled on a sock.

"See how the hole disappears?" he said. "I call it 'trick darning.' "

He laughed a happy, unencumbered laugh such as I was unused to. It had no nervousness in it; it carried no contempt. It stirred a laugh in me I never knew I had.

* * *

Pali sat on the same bench, his ankle over his knee, the same careless look on his face. I might have believed he had not moved since I had first seen him if his clothes had not been different.

"Hello," I said.

"Zoltán," said he.

"I thought we should set up some kind of schedule."

"Sure. Why not come with me for dinner today. We can talk then."

"Well—"

"Well nothing." He stood up. "Meet me here at noon." He walked away, pulling on his cap. "And after, we'll play some soccer," he called.

Pali's house looked like pictures I had seen in my schoolbooks of government buildings. It was gray stone with wide carved steps. As we walked up the steps, I suddenly thought of a white horse coming across a long bridge one cold morning. I had not thought of that in years.

We went into a room our whole house would have fit into. The floors were polished and dark. Three walls were lined with books, floor to ceiling.

"Oh," I said before I thought, "my mother would love this room."

"Really?"

"She reads all the time." I spoke more quietly, for the room seemed to make my voice sound large.

"Take her a book," Pali said with a wave of his hand.

A woman came in carrying a tray. She looked at Pali and he nodded. She laid out cold meats and cheese and lifted a napkin from a bowl of cherries and plums. Then she curtsied to Pali and left without a word.

Pali indicated with a toss of his head that I was to help myself. I began filling a plate, finding myself at ease remarkably quickly.

The plate was light in my hand, and it had a fine gold line around the rim.

"What does your father do?" I asked.

"He's a Reformed pastor in Komárom." Pali took a plate himself. "Cherries, Zoltán?"

"No thanks."

I sat down in a chair of smooth fabric, balancing my plate. I began then, in that dark-walled room, to understand my mother a little. I may even have forgotten where I really belonged, had I not heard, as I set down my book bag, the tiny clink of a tin of shoe polish.

Chapter Five
Planting

"So," said Victor, "you are happy now, I suppose, among your books and professors."

The moonlight made dim outlines of our pillows as it had done since we were very small.

"I like school, if that's what you mean."

"Will you come back here?"

"Of course. Every summer. To work."

"No. I mean after the Gymnásium is done."

"Oh. I don't know. Maybe I'll be back a while." I waited to see where this was going.

"Papa is angry with you, for leaving."

"Yes."

"So why do you go?"

I had tried to answer that question for myself, especially when Pali was stubborn and my own lessons hard.

"Because I have to. Don't you sometimes want more than just planting and milking and falling asleep?"

"No."

"Why not?"

"Because I want to stay here. I'm a good farmer. I like it."

"You can be a farmer and still go to school."

"What for? I already know about farming–more than you, Zoli. What I'd learn in the Gymnásium would be useless here. And what I know here would be useless there."

"That's not true. No knowledge is useless anywhere."

Victor was quiet, but I knew he was angry.

"Do you think you're not smart enough?" I asked.

He snorted and raised up on one elbow. He leaned toward me.

"No, Zoltán, I'm *too* smart. Too smart to be finding out what I'll never use."

"You are a bigger snob than any rich boy I ever saw at the Gymnásium!" My anger flared and surprised even me. "You have to make little what you do not possess and do not understand."

"Think what you like."

"I think what is true. Admit it–you're jealous. And you have no reason. Haven't I always helped–"

"Shut up! Just save your breath, Mr. Knowledge-of-many-things!"

I trembled with the desire to make him see how he gave himself away. A cloud covered the moon, and the room was all but black.

"So stay here," I said. "But it won't make Papa love you any more."

I punched my pillow into a ball under my head.

Victor's silence told me my bullet hit true. And though I felt his pain, I said nothing.

* * *

The Gymnásium was run by the Order of Saint Benedict priests. All students, even the Jews, learned the Roman Catholic prayers because they were repeated so many times. I learned even the Latin prayers as well, out of curiosity.

"Bootblack," as I called the boy I often met on the train–although he was older than I and a year ahead of me in school–was not Roman Catholic either, but he would not learn the prayers.

"Why not?" I asked him. "It's just a thing to learn."

"I say my own prayers to God, Zoli. I don't need some priest to tell me what to say."

The train lurched, joggling us in our seats. My catechism book slid off my lap, and I caught it midair.

"What was that?" I said.

"It happens," said Bootblack. "This engine is overused, Papa thinks."

We were sitting still, but still I could hear the engine. In a moment the train lurched again, and we moved ahead.

"Can you help me with my Latin?" I said when we were rolling again. "You've had this, right?"

"Sure, Zoli. I'd be glad to."

The train jerked along. Its smoke stayed low and blew in our car sometimes. I knew that meant rain. I only hoped it would hold off until after I got to school.

When the train pulled in at Komárom, there was a thin mist everywhere.

"That looks like Professor Kovaly," Bootblack said, leaning down to look out the window.

The professor was indeed standing on the platform when we swung down the train steps.

"Good morning, boys," he said.

"Sir," we said.

"I wonder," he said to Bootblack, "if you'd allow me to walk with Zoltán this morning?"

"Yes, sir," said my train friend, and he slipped away into the fog.

I turned my eyes to the professor, hoping he couldn't read the fright.

"Zoltán, I wanted to tell you how pleased I've been with your work in my classes."

"Thank you, sir." I was only slightly relieved. Surely a professor, even Kovaly, would not walk to the train station to say only that.

"What are your plans, do you think, after you graduate?"

"I want to be a doctor. I want to be"–I sought a word– "useful."

"And you are already," he said. "You are a dependable tutor, from all reports."

But *what,* I wondered.

He stopped walking and looked directly at me.

"I know that it is difficult for you to be in school, though."

I opened my mouth, but he put his hand on my shoulder and spoke ahead of me.

"There's a scholarship coming available that I think you have a good chance of getting. I'd like you to apply for it."

"Really? This is what you came to tell me?"

He opened his eyes wide for a moment and then laughed. It was a rich, rolling laugh, and I found myself smiling, at myself.

"It is," he said. "What did you think?"

"I don't know," I said. "Thank you, sir."

He set off again toward the school. I felt like running all the way to the Gymnásium, but I walked calmly along, not knowing what else to say.

"When the time comes," the professor went on, "you must stay after to meet with the master. Can you do that?"

My heart quickened in my chest. I made, I think, the first real choice I had ever made in my life.

"Yes, sir," I said.

"Good," he said. "Very good."

When the buildings came into sight, I overrode my every instinct and asked him a question.

"Sir," I said, not looking at him, or at anything really. "Why are you so kind to me?"

We took several steps in silence, and I could feel him looking at me.

"Am I so kind to you, you think?"

I could only nod. A drop of rain hit my hand.

"Well, if I am kind, it is because God has been merciful to me. I would be most ungrateful to Him if I were otherwise."

He did not put his hand out to me, but the way he spoke made me feel as though he had.

"Zoltán, do you believe in God?"

The question caught me as though I hadn't studied my lesson.

"Ah, I guess so. I mean I never really thought there wasn't one."

Professor shook his head. "You can be more sure than that, son. I am."

We had come to the classroom building, and I took my opportunity. "I'm sorry, sir. I'll be late. Thank you again, for helping me."

He smiled, but not his usual smile, and held out his hand. I shook it.

He said, "Let me know if I can help you anymore."

I fled to class, just ahead of the rain.

1930

Some people like the spring, they say. I never have. Spring always seemed to bring some kind of pain with it. And even a spring that had no pain carried the ghosts of other years.

This spring was cold and wet. More days than not I was drying my shoes on the train. If the day was not too cold, I walked barefoot to the train and saved on shoe polish.

Bootblack did not come back after the Christmas break. His father was sick, and he had to work. It happened sometimes. Even if you were out only two weeks, you were thrown out of school unless you had been sick and had a doctor's paper.

When the weather finally cleared enough for planting, it was rather late in the season.

"I have two horses and two sowing machines. But I do not have enough sons to help me," my father announced one evening.

"What do you mean by that?" my mother said.

"It takes two to run a sower."

I did not need a Gymnásium education to understand what he meant. He and Béla could run one machine; Victor and I would run the other.

"Zoltán," he said, as though I were somewhere else, "will help here until planting is done."

There was nothing to be said. I had no money to hire someone to replace me. And my father would never agree to hire someone when he had free labor at his command. I could only hope that planting would be finished in a week.

Early next morning we began. Victor and Béla each walked ahead of a horse, pulling a sower. Papa and I walked behind, cleaning the seed tubes. They clogged with mud and the seeds packed up. I wanted to go faster; the horses barely plodded. But speed only made the tubes clog more.

It was tedious work, walking slowly and always bending over. Time upon time we had to stop and reach into the tubes and work the dirt loose. By evening we hadn't planted even half the first field. We worked two hours into the dark, until Béla cried with the pain of holding up his lantern.

I washed my hands at the pump. The water stung my fingers, scraped raw from the seed tubes. When I ate, I held my fork between my second and third fingers, and cared not that the tines had rusted again since morning. At last I picked up the ham and ate it with my fingers. Papa ate only bread.

Victor and I fell into the same bed and slept. We ate at the same table, worked the same fields, pitched hay from the same loft. But we had our separate reasons.

Before light I harnessed the horses with stiff fingers and led them out with a stiff back. We worked without eating or stopping until night fell and the horses stumbled. Béla fell asleep at the table, eating his soup.

The next day was the same. At dusk we lit the lanterns and worked on. At last, on Thursday, while there was still sunlight left, we finished. I threw back my head and laughed.

Chapter Six
Old Songs

"Zoltán, where have you been, son?"

"Professor Kovaly, I–I had to help at the farm. Planting is behind this year."

"Can you catch up four days' work?"

"I think so." I felt my raw fingers. "Yes. I can."

He nodded. "All right. Now, there is the matter of the scholarship I told you about some time ago."

"Yes, sir?"

"I would like you to come to the master's office at three o'clock today. We want to choose between you and another young fellow–Master Padanyi wants to meet you both."

I wondered how I would get back to Szilas in time to do chores. The last train left at five o'clock.

"Yes, sir. Thank you."

I tried to bend my mind to the lessons before me. But I kept thinking of the master's office. I could not imagine what it would look like or what might happen there. So I imagined the outside of the building and the window I knew was the master's. I could not imagine the master either, for I had never seen him.

After history class, I polished my shoes for the second time that day. I brushed my trousers and tried to smooth my shirt. I rolled the cuffs–better to cover the fraying edge than to try to be perfectly formal, I decided.

The rain had stopped, but water dripped from trees and over-hangs, and puddles wavered everywhere. Under the window of one office, some roses had come into bud. The train whistle sounded.

In the master's wing of the building, a man stopped me in the hall. When I told him my purpose, he walked with me to where a heavy dark wood door stood open. Inside I could see three men sitting at a table: Professor Kovaly, an old man with a white beard, and–the tall man with the gold chain who had given me the pants and shoes I was wearing.

A woman in a gray dress told me quietly to sit down, and I took the chair she showed me. Another boy–I had seen him in geography, in the back–sat in a chair to my left. I thought he looked as poor as I did.

I was glad that I had arrived before the master. I looked at Kovaly, but he was talking to the old man.

"Good afternoon, gentlemen," said the man who had given me the shoes. "I am Master Padanyi."

I felt my heart squeeze together into a ball, and then go on beating, but faster now.

"I want to commend you both for your good work in your classes here this first year," he was saying. "And you both are deserving. But we've only one scholarship."

He leaned over to the bearded man and showed him some papers. Then he looked back at us, not sternly, but soberly.

"So I want to hear from each of you. Mr. Hevesi, you first, please."

The boy on my left rose slowly from his chair. I saw that the cuffs of his shirt were frayed too.

"Why have you come to school, Mr. Hevesi?"

The boy cleared his throat. "I–sir–I cannot ask my father for any more money. He doesn't have any. But if I can stay in school, I would like to."

"Why do you want to stay in school?"

He took a breath. "I want to be the town clerk in my village. If I had that job, I could help my family–my brothers and sisters."

"Thank you," the master said.

The boy sat down. I could not tell why, but I felt as though I were looking at some part of myself sitting over there.

"Mr. Galambos."

I stood. "Sirs, I would like to have this scholarship because the only other money I have is what I get from tutoring. Which is enough for tuition, but getting books and paper is sometimes hard. But–"

I felt their surprise at this turn.

"I can probably find a way to make more. I will find a way to stay in school. I cannot bear to leave, now that I've seen how it is to be here."

My face got red. I could feel it. I wanted to explain that I understood this boy beside me, but I stopped.

The master nodded, and I sat down again. He rubbed his hand across his cheek. The three men talked together briefly. The white-bearded man said something that seemed to surprise Kovaly. Then the master turned back to us.

"The gentleman who gives this scholarship would like to hear you sing."

My hands went numb and cold. My breath seemed to be inadequate to fill my lungs.

The master held up his hand as if to quiet us.

"We know that first-year students haven't had music instruction. We just want to hear anything you want to sing."

Hevesi went first. He sang in Latin, in a voice high and clear, like the tune. When he sat down, all eyes turned to me.

The only songs I knew were the Psalms my elementary teacher had taught me. I did not know what Catholics would think of those, but I had nothing else to offer, not even a folk song.

So I stood and sang Psalm 150 as best and as evenly as I could. I came rather quickly to the end.

> *Let all that hath breath*
> *Praise the Lord,*
> *Praise the Lord.*
> *Praise ye the Lord.*

Mr. White Beard did not change his expression. The master nodded for me to sit. Professor Kovaly was looking at me, his eyes full of curiosity.

The master wasted no time. "Gentlemen, thank you for coming. I will be sending you word about our decision in due time. You are dismissed."

Professor Kovaly got up and shook both our hands and wished us well. When Hevesi left, Kovaly held me a moment more. He put forth a small book.

"Here is some reading for the summer. To get ahead on the Greek."

"Thank you," I said. "For everything."

He said I was welcome and went back to the other men.

I looked at the title of the book in my hand: *New Testament.*

* * *

"You're late." Victor did not look up from his milking.

"I know." I thought of explaining, but I didn't. I picked up a hay fork.

"Everything's done." He sounded like Papa, with his shortness.

"Fine." I put down the fork and went to the house.

My mother looked at me, a scowl. I opened my mouth to tell her that I had perhaps a scholarship, but Papa and Victor came in, and she saw only the cooking. We all sat down, and my mother set out the plates.

Papa reached over and took up my plate. He handed it back to Mother.

To me he said, "No chores, no food."

I looked to my mother, thinking she might let me explain. But she would not look at me. I could feel Victor's pleasure in my punishment, in my isolation. I felt as though I did not know these people, as though I had somehow gotten into the wrong house, the wrong time.

I got up and went outside. I started walking back toward the train station. I walked without intending to walk anywhere in particular, like walking in my sleep. Sometime later, I woke up at the station.

The place was empty, but the lamps burned low around the platform. I sat down on the bench, beginning to feel hungry again. Then I remembered the book Professor Kovaly had given me. I felt my pocket. There it was.

I pulled it out and leafed its pages in the lamplight. Some words I could read, but many I couldn't. I flipped back to the beginning.

"The book . . . of . . . something . . . of Jesus Christ."

I knew this name from the catechism.

"The son of David."

There followed line after line of names and then–

"The birth of Jesus Christ."

Suddenly it came to me that this book must be all about Jesus Christ. I did not like history. But Professor Kovaly had given me a book, and for him I would read it. I tried the rest of the page, but the words were hard.

When school ended the last day of June, I went to Kovaly for another favor.

"Would you lend me, please, a Greek lexicon–for the summer?"

The words, once out, sounded horrible. What was I doing asking such a thing? I thought for a second that perhaps I had not even said anything.

Kovaly's smile told me I had. "Glad to, son."

He gave me a grammar as well.

I found Pali with some of his rich friends. I felt shabby, always, in the presence of his friends, and considered not saying good-bye to him.

"Hey, Zoli! You're rid of me for a while," Pali called.

"You're rid of me rather," I called back. Pali had passed into second year, but only barely, and only, I was sure, because I had driven him as I drove myself.

"See you in the fall, professor," he said, and then laughed.

I waved and nodded. Then I walked to the train, trying to memorize everything along the way, in case I never saw it again.

* * *

The harvest was abundant. The wheat came on full in every field. As the fields ripened, the wheat bent down, the kernels hanging in the chaff. The air was clear and dry.

We began at once. Papa and I scythed; Victor and Béla gathered the fallen grain into sheaves. The world dwindled into the width of a swath my scythe made in the standing wheat. *Whish,* and *whish,* and *whish.* My shoulders ached with the repetition. We worked until after eleven o'clock that night.

Papa had us up again at three o'clock. The scythe became a part of my hands by sunup. When my mother brought bread and sausages to us, I could barely uncurl my fingers. Already we were wet with sweat.

Back and forth I swung my scythe, in a rhythm, in a numbing rhythm. After a while I didn't think of the wheat falling to the blade, the blade that gasped with every stroke. I thought of the train, of Bootblack, of Pali, of Pali's house. I thought of Kovaly, of the scholarship, of the book Kovaly had given me.

Mostly, I thought of the book. And some of the words came to me on the rhythm of the scything, like a whispered song, like an ancient song.

Béla and Victor carried the sheaves to the yard, hundreds of sheaves. Long after dark, we leaned the scythes against the barn wall and went in to sleep. Always as I fell asleep, I remembered that in a few days I would be back on the train to Komárom. And I sank away from the pain in my hands on the memory of its whistle.

By some miracle, the reaping was finished one day before school was to start. I had gotten a letter weeks before telling me when to come and what room would be my homeroom. I kept it in the book Kovaly had lent me because I knew Victor would not bother to look there.

"No," said Papa, "you stay for the threshing."

"Why?" I felt a spongy weight in my chest. "Why? You do not need me now!"

My father glared at me, straight across, for I was fifteen now, and tall as he.

"You expect me to pay a stranger, I suppose, to do this work of yours."

"You always pay the harvesters. Every year you give them twelve parts of the harvest for their work."

"I thought I had a man here now. I see that I am wrong."

"You have a man–if you pay him."

My father could not have been more astonished had I hit him.

"Pay you?" He swore at me, and then laughed.

"Will you?"

I thought what I would do if he struck me. And I set my face to cover the racing panic in my veins. The sheaves of wheat around us and the last of the sun were all the reality there was for a long time. Then my father lifted his lip in a sneer.

"Twenty-four parts. For a half-man's work."

Something in me wanted to press the bargain, to get all that was due. Another something held me back.

"Done," I said.

Chapter Seven
Snow on the Harvest

The man with the thresher came the next day, pulling the huge machine behind a steam engine. We were waiting with bags and twine and mountains of wheat. The weather had turned suddenly cool, and clouds began to move in.

The threshing machine swallowed the sheaves, blew out the chaff and straw, and poured out a stream of clean grain. I bagged the grain, holding the sack under the streaming grain time and time again.

I got so I could shake out a bag while the bag under the chute was just starting to fill. Papa took the full bags and tied them off. In spite of the clouds and the breeze, I felt sweat start to run along my hairline.

The dust from the wheat rose like dirty fog. My hands and arms were black; my face felt stiff with the dust that caked in the sweat. I coughed and gasped for air. But I worked on, to show that I was no half a man. My father had to run to keep up with me.

The threshing man weighed the sacks. Then Victor stacked them, crisscrossed on top of each other in two piles–Papa's pile and mine. I turned again and again to see that Victor did not forget–every twenty-fourth bag to one side.

In two days of continuous threshing, I do not remember eating or falling asleep, but I must have. In the end, after the blur of work, I saw in our yard the biggest crop I had ever seen. My part alone was as big as the whole harvest in a bad year.

My father paid the thresher for the use of his machine and thanked him. Then he told us to carry half of both piles into the barn, to feed the cows and to keep for flour through the winter.

"How is that fair?" I said. "The hired men do not give you half of their wages in other years."

"Neither do I feed them, house them, or give them their clothes."

When the excess wheat was sold in the market the next day, my part came to almost a month's tuition at the Gymnásium. I watched as the buyer counted the money to my father.

My father put his money in a leather purse, but he held my money in his hand. He fingered it, at the edges, as though it were fragile. I put out my hand, palm up, to receive it.

He gave it over, slowly. When I had it, I looked up and saw something I had never seen in my life: my father was crying.

Never had I seen him flinch to pay the hired men. But to pay me, I saw, was different. It passed through my head to give him back the money. But I did not. I thought he owed it to me, for many reasons. And I bought myself a shirt and a tin of shoe polish.

* * *

"Hey, Bootblack! You're back."

He smiled his wide smile at me. His teeth were uneven and had gaps between, but it didn't matter.

"Papa is better, and he said to come. My uncle is lending me some money to buy books with. I'm so glad to see you, Zoli. I thought you weren't coming maybe."

I was three days late coming to school because of harvest. I shook off a chill that had come over me, once in the warmth of the train car.

"No, I'm here."

"We might be in the same Latin class now."

"Really? Kovaly's?"

"No, he doesn't teach second-year Latin."

I was sorry, deep in my chest, to hear that.

"What's this you have?" said Bootblack. He pulled the New Testament from the books I was holding.

"Professor Kovaly gave it to me for the summer. To get ahead on Greek."

Bootblack looked squarely at me. "Did you?"

"I did the best I could." I suddenly did not like his interest in this.

"Did you read the book of John?"

"What I could, I told you." I took the book back from him. "I don't like history books. They are just men's opinions, aren't they? I mean, unless a person was there, how can he say what happened?"

"The Bible is not a history book. The Bible is the Bible."

I put the Testament under another book. Bootblack waited for me to say something.

"Oh," I said. "So who does teach Latin second year?"

* * *

The Gymnásium looked, if this is possible, altogether different and exactly the same. There was comfort and welcome in the familiar look of the buildings. But I didn't see any faces I knew. And then I did.

"Pali!"

"Hello, Zoli. Couldn't let go of the plow?"

He called this to me across a lawn.

"Hey," he said. "Kovaly was looking for you."

"Where is he?"

"How should I know? That was three days ago."

The homeroom teacher looked at me with pursed lips.

"Zoltán Galambos?"

"Yes, sir."

"Do you have a doctor's excuse for being late?"

"No, sir." I felt panic rising. I thought the rule was two weeks. It had not occurred to me that for the beginning of school there might be another rule. "I had to stay to help harvest the wheat."

The man opened the attendance ledger.

"Am I still in school?"

"Yes."

I breathed again.

"But each of your teachers will have to permit you into his class. You've missed the fundamentals everywhere."

"What if I can't get into a class?"

"Then you don't get in. You take the class another time."

He did not understand that for me there was no other time. He marked me present and closed the ledger.

I passed into the Slovak language class with little trouble. Pali was in that class, but he ignored me. The geography teacher gave me a map test, and for the second time in my life, I benefited by having taught Victor at home. The Latin teacher did not ask any questions. He merely handed me three days' work and said that if I had it done by the end of the week, I could stay in his class.

The trigonometry instructor, Professor Boniface, did not want me.

"Please, sir, I know I can make up the work, if I have the chance."

"I'm sorry," he said. "You are too far behind. This class moves fast."

His mustache hung down like my father's, and I disliked him for it.

"Please. Give me a chance. I'll show you I can do it."

He paused in collecting his books to look at me. He had brown eyes so dark I could not see the pupils.

"You are very sure of yourself, Mr. Galambos."

I waited, as if at the edge of breaking ice, to see which way the crack would run.

"Very well. Do this problem." He wrote it out and handed the paper to me.

I sat down and looked at the problem. I had never seen anything like it. The numbers swam as I watched them, but I put my pencil to the paper anyway.

"What is your answer?"

"Zero, sir."

"Let me see your work."

I lifted the paper to him as though it were a warrant for my arrest. The edges of his mustache moved as he ran his bottom lip in and out while he studied my paper. At last, I could stand it no longer.

"Is it correct?"

He looked at me from under his black eyebrows.

"No."

I stood up and put back the chair. "Thank you, sir."

"But," he said, stopping me in my turning away, "everything you did was logical. You may enter my class–and if you catch up in a week, you may stay."

"Thank you, sir." I know I smiled, although I generally tried not to, my bottom teeth sticking out so ugly as they did.

The Greek professor turned out to be Kovaly. It embarrassed me how happy I was to see him. But I was happy. So much so that I had to think hard in order not to burst out with some greeting.

He opened his ledger and looked down the rows of seats. Suddenly he saw me.

"Zoltán! Well, here you are, my boy!"

In any other class such attention would have brought contempt down on a fellow from all the others. But Kovaly was so universally liked and so universally kind that no one could suppose he was showing any favoritism.

"See me after class about making up your work."

"Yes, sir."

The hour passed without my knowing it. I did not feel as though I had missed a class; I followed the lesson easily. I suspected Kovaly may have backed up somewhat on my behalf.

I gave him back the books he had lent me over the summer. He took the lexicon and the grammar, but he wrote in the Testament and pushed it back into my hands.

"No, you keep this. Did you read it?"

"Some of it. I'm not sure I translated everything correctly though."

"Well," he said, "let me help you sort it out. Were you able to keep up in class today?"

"Yes, sir. Thank you."

"See there? The extra reading has helped you already. Now, were you able to get into your other classes?"

I told him.

"Good. Very good. Oh, yes, let's see here. I have been keeping this letter for you."

He pulled an envelope from his jacket and held it out.

I opened it slowly, partly because the paper seemed expensive and important and partly because I was afraid. Always I expected the worst.

I read it and could utter only a syllable more like a squeak than a word. I read the paper again.

"I got it! I got the scholarship!"

Kovaly was smiling and clapping my shoulder. "I know. I've been waiting three days to tell you! Congratulations!"

"Thank you. Thank you, Professor." I didn't know what else to say.

"See that you keep up the good work, Zoltán. By the way, you know that you have to take a test on the Heidelberg Catechism next week, don't you?"

"Next week?" I had heard the second-year students talking about it the year before, but I didn't realize the test would be so soon.

Professor nodded. "Do you know any of it?"

"Most of it. I used to read it on the train last year."

"All right. You understand that it is a Reformed catechism, not Roman Catholic?"

I said yes, but I did not really grasp the difference or care about it.

"All the questions and answers are sound, Zoltán. Study beyond what the examination might require, will you?"

"I'll try, sir."

"Good boy. Now show me where you had trouble in the New Testament. Do you have the time? When is your train?"

"In thirty minutes." I had thought of trying to catch up with Pali, but I knew, really, that he would have gone off with his friends already.

Kovaly opened his own Testament. I saw that he had written the margins full. So this was how scholars studied, I thought.

"Can you read this?" He was holding the book out to me.

I pondered the words. "Something about being alive and good things and bad things." I glanced down the page. "I remember this part. I can't understand how this goes–'to be in Christ.' " I looked up at the teacher. "I've got that wrong, haven't I?"

"Not at all. The words say that we will all be judged for what we do while we are alive–whether good things or bad things. And this line says that you can be 'in Christ.' Just as you said."

"I don't understand that translation."

"It is a way of saying that if you believe Christ died for you, you belong to Him."

I must have stared at Professor because he looked up from the page suddenly.

I said, "You believe all this, don't you?"

"I do."

More than the morning of my first day of Gymnásium, I was glad to hear the train whistle in the distance.

When I climbed aboard, the stoker leaned out and called to me. "It's snowing up in Szilas!"

It was only September, and so cold already.

Chapter Eight
Impasse

The snow fell thick. Flakes pattered on my face and stuck to my eyelashes so that I had to keep blinking to see. I walked fast and kept my head down, thinking such big flakes could not make a snow that would last. Mine were the only tracks from the train station to Szilas.

The barn was hushed. From time to time one cow bawled for her calf that my father had sold days earlier. Somehow the smell of hay and grain was heavier in the still of a first snow than in the heat of summer.

I put down straw and fed the horses. For a moment I leaned into the neck of the mare, letting myself feel how tired I was. I may have even slept for fleeting seconds.

"Zoltán! Zoltán!"

I came to instantly. It was my mother.

"Here!" I said. "What is it?"

I found her standing outside the partly closed door.

"Your father! Come to the house!"

Her cotton dress blew around her knees, and she clutched a shawl thrown over her head and shoulders. She looked up at me, and as I stepped out to her, I felt as if I were stepping out of my childhood into a cold unknown.

My father sagged in a chair by the stove, his face turned toward the window. My mother stopped by the table and did not go up to him. She let the shawl drop from her head, careless of the snow that fell.

"Papa?" I approached his chair as I might a wounded animal.

He did not stir or answer.

I went closer, to see his face, his eyes.

"What is it, Papa? Shall I get the doctor?"

At this, he turned his head. "No," he said, more firmly than I would have guessed him able. "No doctor. I am not ready to die yet."

"Help him to the bed," said my mother.

Victor came in much later and ate and sat at the table for a long time, but he never went into Papa's bedroom or asked any questions.

My mother arranged a quilt in an armchair by the bed and sat there. She waved me away, and I gratefully went, leaving her in the dim light of a lamp turned as low as it would go without going out.

Béla came from his room. "What's wrong?"

"Papa is tired," I said. "Let's be quiet, so he can sleep."

"What's wrong, though?"

"Not anything," I said, hoping that would be so.

Béla went back to bed.

"What did you tell him that for?" Victor spoke at last.

"What should I say?"

"Tell him the truth. Tell him Papa worked himself to death."

"That's not the truth."

Victor looked at me as I had seen old men in our village look at Czech soldiers.

"It's not your truth, you mean," he said.

I got up and banked the fire in the stove. I shook the grates and tapped the damper. I would have gone to bed, but Victor was not through with me.

"You see things the way you want so you won't have to quit your precious school."

"What does that mean?"

"If Papa dies, you think you'll have to quit. Well, you won't. I don't need you here."

"Papa isn't dying."

"Of course."

I felt a tightening in my chest, partly anger, partly guilt. I had thought about what my life might become should Papa die. And it was all about the loss of school and my chance at a different life, not about the loss of a father. I picked up the lamp.

"Are you coming?"

Victor did not answer. I think I never disliked him more than at that moment.

"And what are you thinking?" I said. "How you will get the farm if I go away?"

Victor rose out of his chair and came toward me. I still held the lamp; I could feel the heat of it rising to my face.

"I'll show you what I think."

But I only looked at him.

"Come on."

"I'm not going to fight you, Victor. Not now."

He pushed me, and I took a step back. The lamp globe wobbled.

"Don't do it, Victor."

My mother appeared like a ghost, coming quietly into the circle of the lamplight. Her mouth was set, her eyes dark.

"What is this? Did I raise dogs to fight in my kitchen? Go to bed or get out of this house and stay out!"

She held us with a black gaze until we both looked away. The baby wailed suddenly and then settled into a whimpering cry. My mother's face changed only a little, her mouth not making so hard a line.

"See about it," she said to me, and left us.

Victor snatched up the lantern beside the door and went out. I carried my lamp to Dezső, turning down the wick until the flame was just a thin line of light.

Dezső was snuffling in his sleep. His little fists dug into his eyes. He struggled with some dream and then lay still. In a while, his breaths became deep and even.

I went to bed, but I did not sleep. I left the small light glowing in the lamp and watched the pattern it made against the wall. Victor did not come in. I supposed he had gone to sleep in the barn. I put out the light finally and tried in vain to find one comfortable thought to rest my mind on.

I went to the barn earlier than usual and did all the chores that could be done before milking time. Then I milked all the cows that my father always did, leaving Victor's work for him. He came down in a while and set to milking. We saw each other, but our glances never met.

My father was sitting on the edge of the bed. He held a cup between his hands, his elbows on his knees. He did not look up. My mother passed by me and went into the kitchen. I followed her.

"Should I stay here?"

"No, go to school."

She was getting potatoes from a box by the outside door. She held two in one hand and one in the other. With her first finger she knocked off the eyes that stuck out of the two big potatoes.

"But what if he gets sick again?"

"This is a sadness of his, not a sickness."

"What? What happened?"

She looked at me with mild surprise. Then she pulled her lips into a smile that did not reach her eyes.

"Soon enough you will know for yourself, I should think. Life is a burden, and unhappiness is the yoke we pull it by. Everyone comes to know that."

She pushed at an eye in the one potato with her thumb.

"If you are strong, you survive. If you are weak–"

She glanced toward the bedroom.

"If you are weak, you die long before you are buried."

She let the lid of the box slam shut and went to the cupboard to peel the potatoes.

The morning was gray and cold, but the snow had stopped. I fell asleep on the train. Bootblack had to wake me at the station.

It started to snow again, not big flakes this time, but small icy ones that fell like comets.

The Slovak language class was where I was hoping to catch Pali. But he did not come. The teacher called on me to answer while I was wondering whether I still had a tutoring job, and I stood up slowly, hoping that the question would come to me. It did not.

I felt it safer to claim ignorance than inattention.

"I'm sorry, sir. I do not know."

The class burst out in a loud laugh, as if they were one person.

The teacher took off his glasses.

"You don't know how you got here this morning?"

My face burned. I had been asked a simple recitation question.

"I came by train," I said in Slovakian.

"So you do know," the professor said. "Pay attention, Mr. Galambos."

I sat down, my head roaring like a wind inside.

I managed somehow to finish the late Latin assignments between my other classes. When I turned them in, the teacher only flicked his eyes over them and handed them back.

"You might want to check the spelling here–and put your name to your work."

I felt as though I were under all the snow that was falling and the more I tried to get out from under it, the harder it snowed.

Professor Kovaly did not call on me at all in Greek class. His voice wavered in and out of my head, and the book in front of me blurred, then cleared, then blurred again, until I thought I would scream from the effort of staying awake. After ten years, it seemed, the dismissal bell rang.

I took a seat in the train and sank immediately to sleep.

"Zoli. Zoli, wake up."

Bootblack was shaking me.

"My station?" I said, hoisting myself up and trying to get awake.

"No. Are you awake?"

"Stop shaking me. Yes, I'm awake."

I realized that we were not moving and that it was dark outside.

"Where are we?"

"I think about halfway between Komárom and Szilas."

"What happened?"

"We're stalled in the snow, in that little valley with the apple trees."

I saw that a lantern was lit and that the two women in the front of the car had moved to the seat in front of ours.

"How long have we been stuck?"

"About two hours."

"Why didn't you wake me?"

"When the jolt didn't wake you, I figured you needed the sleep. But now it's starting to get cold in here, and you had better stay awake."

I sat fully up and found my shoulder stiff from leaning against the window. I worked my shoulder to loosen it.

"Are you hungry?" one of the women asked me. "I have some apples here."

She held one out to me.

"Thank you."

Bootblack said, "The wheels are probably frozen to the track by now."

"Is it still snowing?"

"It's letting up."

I got up and left the car. I felt my way across the coupling to the next car. There were no people in that one. I felt across another coupling. I got down and walked through snow above my knees and banged to be let into the engine car.

The stoker cracked the door, and I squeezed in.

"Too cold to sleep?" he said, grinning at me.

"How are we going to get out of here?"

"Well, like I told your friend when we first stalled, they'll send a new, stronger engine for us in the morning with a snow plow to dig us out."

"Oh."

"We'll use the steam to keep the cabins as warm as we can."

I was fully awake now. "Will the wood last until morning?"

He didn't answer me.

"Maybe all the passengers should get into one car?" I said.

"Suit yourselves," the stoker said. He scratched his neck under his beard. "The Czechs are in the car back of yours."

He laughed and threw a stick of wood into the furnace.

Bootblack and the ladies were doing some kind of funny dance when I returned. They were in a line in the aisle, jumping from one foot to the other, their elbows linked.

"Come join our drift dance," said Bootblack. "It goes left, right, kick, stop. Then right, left, kick, stop."

We danced the drift dance, and the ladies added more complications to it until the exercise passed beyond my abilities. I fell into a seat, breathing hard.

"Is this called the drift dance because we're in a drift?" I asked.

"No," said Bootblack, "because it keeps you from drifting off to sleep. Now come on."

He pulled me back into the jumping.

Later we ate apples again. Bootblack sliced them up with his pocketknife and handed out the slices.

"Here," he said to the older of the ladies, "is your soup, madam."

She laughed and took it. The next round, he said, as he handed out the slices, was hot sausage.

"And now," he said, his eyes shining, "for the cake!"

He gave each of us a thick slice of apple.

"Eat it slow. Make it last."

Supper over, my mind wandered homeward. I wondered whether they knew the train had stalled or whether they thought I had just not come home. The cold began to edge into my fingers and toes again.

"Let's play a game," said the younger woman. "What shall it be?"

"How about charades?" said Bootblack.

"Oh, yes," said the woman. "That's a good one."

"What is that?" I asked.

"A game my mother plays with us," he said. "You can't say anything. You just act out something, and the rest try to guess what."

He got up quickly. "I'll go first."

He began to make big circles with his arms.

"A bird!" said the younger woman.

He shook his head and carried on his gyrations.

We all laughed at him, and he at himself. I tried to imagine what his mother must be like, to play such things with her children.

"A windmill," said the older woman.

He stopped all of a sudden. "That's right! Your turn now."

"Oh my," she said. "If that's the reward for winning, I'll have to try to lose."

But she got up anyway. We played until the lantern went out and we were left in the dark. Bootblack struck up a song, and we all sang with him.

"You start one," he said to me.

"No," I said, "you had better."

"I thought you got your scholarship by singing."

"I had to sing to get a scholarship, but I'm quite sure I got it in spite of my singing."

"Oh, come," said one of the ladies. "Just think of a song, and we'll join you."

I sighed and gave them the first line of Psalm Fifty.

There was quiet, momentarily, and then a little laugh escaped Bootblack. The ladies giggled. Then we were all laughing.

"Maybe you're right, Zoltán," Bootblack said. "It was probably your good grades that did it for you."

Deep in the night, I realized that everything had been quiet for some time.

"Bootblack," I said, "wake up."

"I'm not sleeping, Zoli," he said. "I'm praying."

His words thrust fear up in my chest.

"Why?"

"I always do. Right now I'm praying for my family, that they won't worry about me, and for us that we will be all right until the plow comes. And for your family–"

His words jerked at me like hands.

"And for you."

I wished I could see his face. "You don't need to pray for me," I said.

I couldn't tell why I said it.

Chapter Nine
Coming Awake

The engine with the plow came an hour after daybreak. It pushed us back to Komárom, clearing the track as it went. The sun was back, a September sun, warm and yellow, and already it seemed impossible that we had feared freezing to death only the night before.

Bootblack took the train home from Komárom as soon as there was one. I stayed and went to school, since I was behind several days work as it was.

In the evening, I had a momentary uneasiness as I boarded the train, but sleep was stronger, and I woke up in Boda, the station at Szilas.

Papa was in the barn, milking as usual; Victor was feeding the calves.

"The train got stuck in the snow," I said to both of them at once. "Just below Komárom."

Neither said anything. I left without doing any chores and went to the house. My mother met me at the door.

"Where were you?" she said.

"The train couldn't come through the snow last night. Had to wait on a plow."

I smelled broth, and I felt faint.

"I need to eat," I said.

I had soup and bread, and I drank five glasses of milk. My stomach full, the warmth of the stove spreading through me, I suddenly felt weighted down with weariness.

"I'm sorry. I have to go to bed."

"Go."

The next thing I heard was my mother saying, "You'll miss the train, Zoltán."

I rolled over and opened my eyes. It was light. I sprang up to grab my school clothes and was instantly dizzy. My head felt full of water, and my knees gave out. I sat down, looking at my feet, which seemed not to belong to me anymore.

I took several deep breaths and stood up slowly. My head ached and seemed too heavy to hold up. It was so cold in the room that I decided to dress in the kitchen.

My mother had set bread and cheese on the table; all the other dishes had been cleared away. My hands were so cold I could hardly cut the cheese. But my face felt hot, as though I had been tending the fire all morning.

I put on one of my old shirts under my school shirt. I put on my heavy coat as well. On the walk to the train station, I saw the sky was clearing. I thought that I should not need my heavy coat, but the idea of taking it off made me shiver.

Trigonometry was impossible for me. I couldn't hold my mind to it. All I wanted to think about was finding a place to lie down and sleep. Professor Boniface's voice sounded as if he were talking down a well or as voices do when you're just falling asleep.

Kovaly's Greek class was easier. I could follow the reading, because much of it came from the New Testament. As the hour passed, a sense of panic began to grow in me, but I could not tell why. My heart beat faster; my breaths came short.

A compulsion to stand and leave came over me. My training told me not to. The struggle made me dizzy. I raised my head. Professor Kovaly was talking still but looking at me intently. I saw him stop talking. I felt several students turn in my direction. As I stood up, I thought I saw Kovaly coming toward me. And then all light and sound were sucked out of the room, and I fell into the dark.

* * *

There was a thin white curtain over the window, but I could see that the sky was bright blue. Still the curtain confused me because I could not remember it.

"Zoltán?"

It was a woman's voice, but not my mother's. I looked toward it. A woman with gray hair pulled back from her face sat leaning toward me, smiling.

"Hello," she said. "How do you feel?"

I did not know. I really did not feel like anything.

"Where am I?"

"You're at Professor Kovaly's house. I am Mrs. Kovaly."

I saw the white quilt draping over me. I pulled my arm out from under it and saw that it was covered with a sleeve that I did not recognize. An understanding, a horrible understanding, began to wash in on me.

"What day is this?"

"It's Sunday, Sunday afternoon."

I sat up, too quickly, for having lain down for three days.

"No, no." She was standing now, her hand on my shoulder. "You just wait now. Let me tell Henrik you're awake."

The professor came in, not wearing his jacket. It seemed so strange to see him in shirt sleeves that I forgot what I wanted to say to him. His wife came in with him, but she stayed back by the door.

"How are you, my boy? You had quite a time of it."

I could not speak. The more I understood, the more I wanted to be gone from there.

"Would you like something to eat?" Mrs. Kovaly said. "How about some soup?"

I wanted soup, but I did not want to have these people do any more for me.

"Yes," said the professor. "Let's have a little broth here."

She went out, leaving the door ajar.

"What happened?" I did not want to hear, but I had to know.

"Well, you fainted in class. You stood up as though you would say something and then just went down."

I had come to that on my own. What I meant was, what had happened here, in this house. I did not know what to say. How could I look this man in the eye again?

He was going on. "And since there was no way you could travel, I told some boys to carry you here. You have been quite sick, Zoltán. You were in and out of delirium until yesterday."

I looked down at my nightshirt. Right then I was far more concerned about details other than my health.

Kovaly smiled his smile. "My wife has been looking after you. She's the best there is."

The humiliation I felt then could not have been worse. I did not want that woman to come back into the room, ever.

The professor poured a glass of water from a pitcher by the bed. He offered it to me.

"We have two sons grown and gone," he said. "My wife knows how to take care of boys. But not to worry, Zoltán; I saw to certain things myself. All right?"

If ever I had been grateful to Kovaly, it paled beside this new gratitude.

I ate the soup Mrs. Kovaly brought me. Kovaly told me that he had sent word to my parents with Bootblack and that my father had sent money back with Bootblack.

"You'll take most of that back to him. I'll keep a bit, so as not to insult your father."

I sighed at the prospect of explaining at home. Kovaly studied me.

"But we'll talk about this later," Kovaly said. "Are you tired? Shall I leave you to sleep?"

Suddenly the thought of his leaving the room made me vastly lonely.

"No. Please stay."

"All right," he said.

He talked about how I would catch up in school and how the other boys asked about me. By and by he read to me from the Bible until I fell asleep.

Later in the evening Mrs. Kovaly brought more soup and some warm bread.

"I warmed the bread in the oven. I thought you might like that."

"Thank you. Thank you for everything."

"It's quite all right. My husband loves all you boys so that I just think of you as more sons. So don't you trouble yourself to thank me anymore. Here's some water. Try to drink all you can, will you?"

Her hair shone in the lamp glow, like a white light around her head. I took the glass from her. I had to hold it in both hands.

"And don't be thinking of going to school tomorrow. You're going to stay here. We've got all your books, and you can read a little, if you don't get too tired."

All the while she laid out my life for the next day, she changed pillowcases and straightened the bedcovers.

"Now, there's everything you need right here. But if you want me, you just call. We're only across the hallway. All right?"

"Yes, thank you."

"All right. Good night, son. Sleep well."

"Good night."

She blew out the lamp and left quietly, as though I might already be asleep.

I could hear their quiet voices in the other room. Once in a while, Kovaly's words were clear to me, as though he passed the cracked door as he spoke. Then his voice became a murmur.

He said once, "We must pray about that." And I thought I heard my name. I closed my eyes and went to sleep on the rise and fall of their voices.

* * *

For several more days, I mostly slept, ate the stews and breads that Mrs. Kovaly brought me, and waited for Professor to come in during the evenings.

"Hello, Zoltán. How are you today? You're color is back, I see."

"Yes, sir. Thank you. I feel well enough to go home, I'm sure."

"Well, we'll see."

He sat down in the chair by the bed, but he did not go on about the other boys at school or ask about my reading. He leaned forward, his elbows on his knees, and his hands clasped.

"Son, I haven't told you something because I didn't want you to worry about it. And I don't want you to worry now."

He looked up at me, not sad, but not smiling.

"Pali has gotten into some trouble, and his father sent him away. It makes me very sorry for him. But you have nothing to worry about–your scholarship should cover everything until we find you another tutoring job."

He smiled then.

"Yes," I said.

I wanted to know what Pali had done, where he had been sent, if he was coming back. And I wanted to say that I didn't know how I would have enough money for everything.

"All right," said the professor, as though he had not said anything terribly important, "let's do a little reading, shall we?"

In the morning, Mrs. Kovaly let me get up and come downstairs to read. The room I sat in was full of light from many windows. I worked on my geography. Mrs. Kovaly was humming and singing softly to herself in the kitchen.

There were pictures of people on the walls. One was of Kovaly and his wife, their hair dark and their faces smooth, and three children, two boys and a girl.

When she came in with some tea later, I was looking at it.

"That was taken thirty years ago," she said. She went to the oval glass and polished it with her apron.

"These are Joseph and Aaron, our sons. And this was Elizabeth. She died soon after this picture was taken."

She turned to me and smiled. "Have you ever read of Queen Elizabeth of Hungary? She was so kind and beautiful. I named Elizabeth after her."

She stayed to have tea with me. Once or twice when she spoke of her husband, her face brightened so that I nearly turned to see whether he had come in.

I went to school from Kovaly's house two days later and then took the train home. Although I got tired on the train, I felt that I had slept enough.

My mother and Béla walked down the lane to meet me.

"Were you very sick, Zoli?"

"Yes, Béla." I looked at my mother. "But I'm all right now."

Béla said, "I help with chores now. I feed the calves."

"Good for you." I wanted to ask about Papa, but I could not with Béla there.

My mother said, "Are you hungry?"

"I could eat."

My father did not say anything. He nodded to me, as though I were someone he infrequently met in the village. I gave him the money Kovaly wanted returned to him. He counted it.

"Did he keep enough?"

"He is an honest man," I said.

Life went back to chores and trains and classes, chores and trains and classes. I learned all I could while I sat in class. My father had taught me the power of learning by watching at least. I read on the train and studied in what free hours I had at school. Only when I was doing chores was my mind free to wander to other things than schoolwork.

Much of the time I tried to think of ways I could get more money for school. It scared me to think of giving up what I had come to believe was the only way out of a life like my parents'.

I thought a great deal about what I had observed in the Kovalys' house. I remembered how Kovaly smiled when his wife came into the room or when he even heard her coming. I went over and over again in my imagination the little kindnesses Mrs. Kovaly had done, like warming the bread and leaving the door ajar.

I remembered hearing the two of them praying together, and then I would always think of Bootblack praying on the train that night. I put the pieces together every way I could, to make an explanation, to find a reasonable reason for Kovaly's gentle generosity and Bootblack's apparent happiness in the face of poverty like mine. Always the conclusion was the same: either these people were completely wrong or they were completely right.

Bootblack, the wisest, kindest friend a person could have, had never lied to me or even tried to trick me. He was as happy for my getting a scholarship as though he had gotten it himself. He was more a brother than any that sat at my father's table.

No one not insane himself could question Kovaly's hold on reality. Of all my professors, he was the one least wound up in his subject, and yet he was the best teacher. He cared for the people in front of him, not his position or his intellect, and what better proof of sanity was there?

Neither could I doubt anymore his sincerity. Not since I had been in his house, not since I had received only goodness at his hands at all times, not since I had watched him in public and private–both when he knew he was watched and when he didn't–and had seen the same man.

Yet what I knew of life was all too real as well, and somehow more convincing. My mother was right: life was a burden. All a person could do was try to be strong enough, to hold out for the quiet moments between the terrors. I could not reconcile the two realities.

"Where is your head?"

My father's voice came from the left of me.

I suddenly became aware that I had been standing with a pitchfork in my hand for some time, doing nothing. I went back to work without answering. Victor carried two full pails away, looking at me as he might at someone who had stolen from him.

"His books make him sog-headed," he said.

I put up the fork. I followed Victor, and when he had emptied a pail, I took it.

"Leave that," he said.

"I was going to finish up," I said.

"I don't need any help."

I tossed the pail down, and it rolled in his direction.

That morning, November seventeenth, I walked to the train as usual, thinking again about things, when something made me stop. I stood there in the road, my book bag over my shoulder and my breath carrying white on the still air.

The road wound before me and curved out of sight. Suppose, I thought, that Kovaly was wrong about everything–was his life then wasted? My whole self sprang to his defense at the thought. Suppose my mother was right. The ache that came with this tack bowed me with an awful weight.

What was the essential difference in the two ideas? Both seemed to acknowledge that pain and sorrow came with life. But unlike my mother's view, Kovaly's did not deny that joy and hope also came with it. How could Kovaly believe in joy and hope even in pain and sorrow?

"Dear God, I want to know what Kovaly knows. I want to know what it is to be a Christian."

The sun came up over the trees as I stood there, and I had the feeling suddenly that I had been asleep all my life and that this clear November morning was the first morning I had ever really been awake to see. I let the bag slide from my shoulder.

Life, I thought, *is* a burden–but only to those who try to carry it all themselves. That was the piece that made all the others fall into line. That piece accounted for my mother's view, which seemed true. But it also explained how a man like Kovaly could know life and still be happy.

"I know I am not worthy of Your help, but I don't want to go on by myself. I want to–"

I stood on the empty road, as though the rest of the world had dropped away, as though I spoke to God from a wasteland.

"To be in Christ, if You will have me."

I felt that the words traveled out in all directions over the white fields around me, like light snow whirling across the top of frozen ground, lifting with the slightest wind.

The train whistle sounded, but it did not call me this time. I snatched my bag up and went home faster than I ever had in my life. I thought only to tell Mama that I had found a better yoke to pull life by.

Part II

NOBODY'S BOY

1933-1937

When my father and my mother forsake me,
then the Lord will take me up.

Psalm 27:10

Chapter One

Men and Boys

1933

"And, Father, we pray again for Zoli's Mama and Papa and his brothers. If it be Thy will, please let them come to understand You love them. Now, we ask for grace in our classes. Help us not to make Thee ashamed. Amen."

Bootblack's strong amen carried down the green hill to the Gymnásium. He seemed so much a man already, at eighteen, leading us.

"Amen," five of us said together.

There was a moment; then Szabo said, "I had to tell Dr. Boniface I didn't have my work done today."

"Well," said Bootblack, "you didn't lie. That's good."

"Yes, but I didn't have the work done."

"I can help you," I said.

"Oh, I understand it all right. I just didn't do it."

No one said anything. I understood; we all did. Time ran out on us or sleep overtook us or other things rose up in front of school.

Bootblack started a song. His deep voice was warm as the day. The elm we sat under stretched over half the lawn behind the classroom wing.

Later we got up and shook hands all around and went to class.

"Well," said Professor Boniface, as we passed by under the window of his office, "will the Reformed presbytery be meeting today, Reverend Galambos?"

I looked up. His mustache still hung down, but now he wore glasses over those dark eyes. The gold cross around his neck glinted at us.

"We already met," I said.

He snorted and drew the window closed.

"Never mind," said Bootblack.

"I don't."

"Look," he said, not waiting for me to read the letter he held out, "it's from the orphanage in Farna. They need help a couple of weeks this summer. What do you think?"

I said, "You would be good at that kind of work."

"No," he said, "I mean do you think you could help? I want to go, sure. But I want you to come too."

"Me?"

He laughed. "What's the matter?"

"Nothing. It just surprises me, is all."

"So think about it. Where were you this morning?"

"Talking to Hevesi. Or trying to."

"I asked him last week to come to our Bible study."

"He won't come. He still holds it against me, I think–that I got the scholarship we both were up for three years ago."

Bootblack nodded. He folded the letter and stuffed it into the book he was carrying.

"It could be only that he's Jewish, you know. Doesn't want to be seen with Christians."

"No, it's me that keeps him away. I wish he would see me differently now."

Bootblack and I walked in silence for a minute.

He said, "I have to study this Roman history, or I'll be seeing my grades differently. Will you be on the early train?"

"Yes."

A new student passed by us and spoke to us in Czech. I answered in Czech.

"I know that fellow from the train station," I said. "He's from Pribeta."

"Pribeta!" Bootblack swung around to look at the boy again. "Then what's he doing speaking Czech to us?"

There was one thing that many of us did not see differently: Czech rule. When I sat in the Czech language class, when I saw the Czech soldiers on the train, when I saw my nationality on Gymnásium registration declared Czechoslovakian, I felt cold, as though the world had only gray November days left to it.

"Maybe we look Czech to him."

Bootblack thumped me with his book.

I said, "We learned Czech, too, you know."

"That's different entirely. I know Latin too, but you don't hear me talking it in my sleep."

"Don't let Professor Kovaly hear you say that," I said.

But Bootblack would not be nudged into his usual good humor again.

"The Czechs are subtle," he said, thumbing the pages of history in his hand. "They would rather wear us down than meet us head on. And they are wearing us down, taking over the schools and making the children learn Czech."

"No one can wear Hungary out of a Hungarian. We might learn their language, but we will never be Czech."

Bootblack made a thin line of his mouth.

I said, "Horthy will put Hungary back together–I believe that. I think I have always believed that."

"Yes, you've told me before of the regent and his white horse on the bridge at Budapest."

"Horthy may be many things you don't like, but he is no Marxist."

"Let us hope. I'll see you on the train."

* * *

Spring seemed warmer than I had ever remembered. The cherry trees puffed with blossoms and dissolved into green and hung with hard little promises of cherries before I had even noticed. Béla now stole the fruit from Grandfather's trees when the chances came to him.

"Stealing is wrong, Béla, no matter how many right reasons you think you have."

He stood looking down at the stains on his hands and running his tongue out of the corner of his mouth.

"It's not worth it. I told you what happened to me, taking cherries."

I reached up and rubbed my jutting jaw, like some old man. Forever I carried it, the mark of early disobedience.

Victor passed by without stopping, but he nodded a wink at Béla.

Béla smiled back at him, and my words, I could tell, were beginning to pull apart in his brain like clouds in a summer sky.

"Stay out of the trees," I said.

I went to brush the horses. Their winter coats were rolling off them in basket loads. The smell of horse and damp air made me think of planting.

"What do you preach at Béla for?" Victor said. "Can't you just save that for your sissy friends at school?"

"No."

"Well, Papa–"

"Papa wasn't there."

"Doesn't matter. He told you to leave your Bible talk at school, didn't he?"

I made short hard strokes down the shoulder of the horse, and the dust and dry hair flew.

"Well, didn't he?" Victor persisted.

"Is it preaching to tell your brother not to make the mistakes you did? To tell him of the danger? If it is, I might say that you were preaching to me just now."

Victor glared at me. And I felt a pang at bringing up that look.

"Let's not always fight," I said. "I don't–what can I do that would make you believe me? I don't hate you."

Victor's mouth curled up in a nasty smile.

"That's too bad," he said. "It makes you weak."

"What does that mean? What has weakness to do with anything?"

He walked away. The horse shook its mane and pulled a mouthful of hay from the rack. I gave the back and sides a few more swipes and quit. I knew what Victor meant, somewhere in the back of my brain. But I could not convince him that I had long ago given over the contest for Papa.

Papa hardly spoke at all any more, to any of us. My mother read more books to escape the silence and the endless round of work. Victor worked like a machine on the farm, day and night. I did not remember Papa working as incessantly, even in the worst of times.

"What are you doing," I asked him one night, "working so hard all the time? Even Papa rests sometimes."

He hung his hat on a peg by the door.

"I'm doing what needs to be done."

"Meaning my part, I suppose?"

"Meaning nothing. Work is work."

Victor never did anything without a reason. He meant to get somewhere with this ceaseless toil, I was sure. It was the old battle still. And he would not let me withdraw my forces. He always held me at the front line with his scorn.

"That's right," I said. "Work is work."

I turned over the page I had been writing on. Victor looked at me as if from a great distance.

Our mother looked up from her book, first at Victor, then at me. She put the silk bookmark that had belonged to her father between the pages and closed the covers. She held the book out so that the gold letters showed in the lamplight: *Beyond Good and Evil*.

"Have you read this?" she asked me.

"No. What is it?"

She felt for the hairs that had come loose around her face. She tilted the book toward herself. Victor strode past and went to bed.

"A book by a man who knows what life truly is." She smiled at me, thinly. "You should read it."

"I have a Book that tells me truly what life is, Mama."

She stood up. I thought she would tell me yet again that Christianity was only for the weak. But she did not. For a moment it seemed as though she might reach out and touch my cheek as she had once when I was very, very small.

"You are so young," she said. "I cannot remember being so young."

I took a breath to answer her, but she was gone, out of the lamplight, out of hearing.

It was quiet in the house, and without. I could feel my heart beating, hear it almost, as though I were the only person alive. How easy it was to imagine that I was alone.

I remembered about the orphanage. I wondered how much different an orphan's life could be from mine.

* * *

My legs ached from pumping the bicycle up what had to be the longest hill in Hungarian Czechoslovakia.

"How–*puff*–far–yet?" I said.

"To the top–" said Bootblack, "or to Farna?"

"Farna," I gasped.

"Only two or three kilometers."

I felt as though that might as well be three hundred.

"All uphill–*puff*–I suppose."

"Come on, Zoli. You're a farmer."

I wanted to point out that he was used to riding bicycles, and that these were the bicycles he was used to, and that, after all, farming was not the best training for fifty-kilometer bicycle trips, but I could not spare the breath.

At Farna, I remember wobbling through the streets on the bike and being told at last to sit down on the worn steps of the orphanage kitchen. A tall, aproned woman brought me water and some cooked cherries. I could only sit and hold the glass and the bowl.

"That's Mrs. Vrabel," said Bootblack. "She's the cook here. And you had better eat what she brings you."

I nodded, for I could still feel the vibration that the force of her steps had made on the planks. I forced the spoon to my mouth.

In minutes she was back to collect the bowls and glasses.

"Pastor Toth wants to see you boys right away. You can leave your bicycles here a little. But you will want to put them up before the children come in."

"Thank you," said Bootblack. "And thanks for the cherries. They were very good."

"Oh, be off with you," said she. "Pastor's waiting in the meeting hall."

I would have taken Toth for a farmer, not a pastor. He was big and square, with a booming voice. He shook our hands as though they were plow handles in want of steering.

"Let's go meet the children," he said. "We have just two days until the conference starts, and I'll be wanting you two to be in charge of the children by then."

The children, all boys, were running wild in a field, their shouts and laughter punctuated occasionally by the hollow *ponk* of a soccer ball.

"That's soccer?" I said to Bootblack.

Pastor Toth said, "Well, it's their version of it. I don't think it hurts anything to let them play their own way. Boys!"

His voice thundered out over the field and instantly thirty boys were running toward us. I had a moment's thought of taking cover, but I realized they were all coming straight for Toth. They swarmed around him, ran into him, clamored to tell him about a hundred things.

Toth, like a big tree in flood waters, waved his arms and called for quiet. In a while, there was quiet, or something close to it, and he put his arms down.

"Now, then," he said, "while I am busy with the Bible conference, these two men are in charge."

I felt suddenly much older and taller than ever I had. The boys' faces turned to us.

"This is Mr. Nandor," he said. "And this is Mr. Galambos. You must do as they tell you. Now say their names to me."

Our names were shouted back at us in a jumble of noise.

"All right," said Toth. "Back to your game."

The eddying pool reversed itself and flowed back onto the field.

"They're a bit hard to handle. But I hate to be too harsh with them. Their lives have been so unhappy, you know."

I watched the ball rise into the air and all the boys slow to follow its arc and be ready when it fell again. Toth and Bootblack talked together about the conference. A light wind swept past, cooler up here than in Komárom. There was a heaviness bowing me down, and I felt like walking away.

"So," Toth was saying, "then your job is to keep some order and make sure the boys eat and study and wash up as they should. And try to talk to them as much as you can about the Lord."

Bootblack said, "All right."

I just nodded.

Supper was served at six. Mrs. Vrabel somehow produced chicken and boiled cabbage for thirty-five, carried the food out in huge dishes, and kept order at the tables. For a while all that could be heard was the clattering of forks and plates. Then as the boys' stomachs began to get full, the talking and the laughing grew to a roar.

Mrs. Vrabel drummed on a metal washtub with her wooden spoon.

"No shouting in my kitchen," she said.

A little boy about Dezső's size climbed off his bench and made for the door. Mrs. Vrabel took two strides and caught him by the collar.

"Where do you think you're going? Sit down and eat your supper, young man."

He scrunched up his face and wailed. She smiled a little and bent down to him. He continued to wail. Then she kissed him soundly on the cheek and scooped him up like a sack of potatoes. She carried him sobbing, sideways on her hip, and landed him back in his place at the table.

"Won't do a bit of good, Dani," she said. "Eat your peas."

The hall had become quiet during this exchange. Now all that we heard was the snuffling resistance Dani made over his plate and Mrs. Vrabel's footsteps back to the stove. A few snickers erupted here and there, and soon we all were laughing.

"All right," said Toth, standing up. "If you're finished, go on out and use up the daylight that's left."

The hall cleared, and I noticed that Dani was among the exodus.

"Do you mind helping clear up?" Toth said to us. "My wife usually does, but she's sick tonight."

"I was expecting to," said Bootblack, reaching for one last roll. "Be glad to."

"That's the way," said Toth. He clasped me on the shoulder and leaned close, as if to tell us a secret.

"Just tonight, I should think," he said. "Because tomorrow Mrs. Vrabel's daughters come in from Leva for a visit."

He ducked his chin and winked, as though we were all party to some information that no one was mentioning aloud. He slapped my shoulder again and was off.

"Girls?" I said. I picked up a plate and scraped its remnants onto another with a piece of half-eaten bread.

"It's not what you think, Zoli," said Bootblack. "They're little girls. They come here every year during conference, to be with their mother. They go to school up north in Leva."

"Oh." I could not tell which was greater in me–relief or disappointment.

"Let's wash these, too," he said. "It's seems enough to me that she cooks all this food."

"Sure."

It was dark by the time we had the kitchen put back together.

"Thank you, boys."

In this domain, we were suddenly boys again. But I did not feel younger.

Mrs. Vrabel hung the damp dishtowels on a clothesline above the sink.

"Thanks for supper," I said. "It was good."

"Oh, go on with you, now," she said. "You've got plenty to do yet tonight."

The dormitory was vibrating with noise as I knew it would be.

"Hey," I yelled. "Hey!"

There was a momentary lull.

"I have a deal for you fellows."

The novelty seemed to quell them.

"Here it is. I know how to play soccer–real soccer. And I'll teach you–we'll have teams and everything–but–"

The wave of eagerness that had surged toward me crested on that last word.

"But–you have to do a thing for me."

The wave paused at curl, and hung there, neither breaking on shore or rolling back under.

A voice said, "What?"

"At every meal for the next two weeks, you will line up with your dirty plates, scrape them into the barrel, and stack them on the drain board for Mrs. Vrabel."

The wave rolled under with a groan.

"Fine," I said. "It's your choice. I just thought you'd like to play soccer like the big boys at the Gymnásium in Komárom."

"Time for prayers," said Bootblack.

I could not tell, but I thought at lights out, I could hear another wave of enthusiasm coming toward shore.

Chapter Two
Challenge

Breakfast was more subdued than supper, owing probably to the early hour. Bootblack and I glanced at each other over our food, both of us thinking the same thing.

My legs and shoulders were stiff from the long ride. I almost hoped that the boys would reject my deal. A morning of soccer with thirty small boys seemed beyond me.

Presently one of the larger boys stood, took his plate to the barrel, and scraped it off. Then he carried it to the sink. Mrs. Vrabel looked at him as though he must be up to something. Another boy followed him, and a line formed. The first boy stood by the sink, like a sergeant with recruits.

"What's this?" said Pastor Toth.

"A test," I said.

"Zoli told the fellows that he would teach them to play soccer if they would carry their dishes up after meals."

"Well, well," said the big man. "Who would have thought that would work?"

Bootblack and I went to the field. We managed to divide the boys into fairly evenly matched teams. There were eight boys left.

"What about making fifteen-man teams?" Bootblack said.

"No, we have to do this right. We'll just tell the others that they will play later and give them other jobs for now. Like scoring or judging."

Bootblack looked doubtful, but he did not argue.

"Remember which team you're on," I said. "Now before we play, we have to practice some skills. We'll start with kicking."

Up and down the field for an hour they went, trading off the ball, dribbling around Bootblack and me, until I could see which of them were possible captains.

"All right," I said. "Get some water and then have a rest."

We worked on passing the ball for another hour. Then Bootblack showed them how to head a ball, and I showed them how to be a goalie. When every boy had tried being a goalie at least once, I called for a game.

I assigned two goalies and two center forwards, and Bootblack stationed the rest in positions on the field. I put two boys at each end of the field to judge the goals. I sent one to the center to call the opening play. Bootblack took two boys with him to be officials. Dani, the escapee from supper, became my charge.

"What's my job?" he asked.

I looked down.

"You must keep the score."

"Will it go higher than ten?"

"Very likely."

"But that's all the farther I can count."

"Then today will be the day you learn to count higher."

He gazed up at me and then broke into a huge grin.

"If you were my uncle, I could call you Zoli *bacsi*."

"We'll see."

Dani needn't have worried about his numbers. Before five minutes had passed, the center forward of one team slammed into the goalie of the other team, and they came up swinging. Bootblack pulled off the goalie and held him.

I tried to hold the forward by the elbows, but he broke free with one arm and landed a punch in my side. I had him flat on the ground with his arm up behind him before I had even thought.

"Zoli!"

Bootblack's voice came to me from very near. I sat back on my heels and let the boy up.

"Don't try that again," I said.

The boys were quiet, looking at me. The forward pulled himself to his feet. His shirt was grass-stained, his face red.

"Everyone just go sit down," Bootblack said. "We won't play again until you can behave."

The boys melted away to the sides of the field. Some of them sat; some of them stood.

"He said sit down!" I hollered at the rebellious.

Slowly they all sat down.

"Are you all right?" Bootblack said.

"Of course."

"Shall we go on, do you think?"

"Let them worry a little while," I said.

"You don't have to be so hard on them."

"Somebody should be."

Bootblack said nothing. We just stood together on the field until we felt like calling for another game.

* * *

There they were, the daughters. Two of them were little girls, as Bootblack had said. The other two were not.

"Little girls, huh?" I said to Bootblack.

"They were," he said, "last summer."

The tallest of them had thick braids wrapped round her head. The skirt of her gray school uniform blew around her knees as she stood on the porch of the kitchen.

"She's looking at you," Bootblack said.

"No, she's looking at you."

"Go say something to her."

"Why don't you?" I said.

"Because she's looking at you."

"Well, you know her, don't you?"

A voice, Mrs. Vrabel's, ended our quandary.

"Ilona, Anna, come in here."

The gray uniform and the braids went inside. The door bounced twice and then stayed shut.

"Why didn't you go say something?" I said.

"Same reason you didn't."

Bootblack elbowed me. I pushed him back.

"That's Margarette," said Mrs. Toth at our table later. "The blonde. And the little one is Editke."

The thick brown braids were coming toward our table. The girl set a pitcher down in front of Bootblack and smiled at him. It made me think of the sunlight under the elms, the way she moved.

"And that's Ilona," said Mrs. Toth.

"I see," I said.

I realized too late that I had buttered my bread on both sides. Mrs. Toth laughed. "You see, do you? I see too."

Bootblack's cheeks were also red, but he was speaking.

"Your mother is still a good cook."

"Yes, she is."

Her voice was light and gentle.

"This is my friend."

She turned her gaze to me.

"Zoli–Zoltán–Galambos. He's from Szilas. We go to the Gymnásium in Komárom together."

"Hello, Zoltán."

"Hello."

"This is Ilona Vrabel."

She smiled and looked down, and I was grateful, for I had nothing to say. I put my hand to my chin.

She said to Bootblack, "I have to get back to work."

When she walked away, I thought of the little roses under the master's window at the Gymnásium. I wondered whether any grew here.

"She is the oldest," he said to me. "Anna is next."

I only nodded. It had never occurred to me, but as I looked at Bootblack, I realized that he was handsome, despite his crooked teeth.

Mrs. Vrabel was suddenly there with a plate of bread.

"I'll have plenty of kitchen help, boys. No need for you to stay tonight."

* * *

"Listen," I said. "I hear music."

Bootblack rolled over on his back and listened. The moonlight shone in on him, but it missed my bed altogether.

"Must be Ilona. She plays the mandolin."

He rolled back and reworked his pillow.

The tune was so soft I couldn't hear many of the notes. Still it held me awake. It ended soon after, and though I waited a long time, she never played again.

"Zoli bacsi. Zoli bacsi."

"Wha–"

"Zoli bacsi, I'm sick."

I was awake now. The moon was down; the little face next to my bed was barely visible.

"What's the matter? Is that you, Dani?"

"I'm sick."

I kicked my feet out and sat up.

"Sick how?"

"I have a stomachache. Can I sleep with you?"

I rubbed my face to think. My internal clock told me it was a long way from morning.

"Let's get a drink of water and see if that helps."

He drank the water, and I studied him in the lamplight. He did not look pale. I pushed his hair back off his forehead, but he did not feel hot.

"Maybe it was a bad dream," I said, thinking of Dezső, who used to struggle in his sleep sometimes.

"Maybe." The voice was smaller than the boy.

I took him to his bed, and when he was in it, I blew out the lamp. But even as I lay down to sleep again, I could still see how he had looked at me, not wanting to be left. I jerked the sheet over myself. I should not have come, I thought.

* * *

She was hanging clothes out. The sheets billowed, and she appeared for an instant and disappeared again.

"Mr. Galambos," a boy called, "you're not looking."

I turned back to the field.

"Yes, I am. You're doing much better."

"But the ball went out-of-bounds and you didn't call it."

"Joseph is the official this morning. He knows to call it."

"You have to help," the boy insisted.

"I'll do better than that. I'll play forward, if Mr. Nandor will play forward for the other team."

The boys cheered. They swarmed around Bootblack, calling for him to accept. Bootblack questioned me with his look, but he gave in to the pleading around him.

I took the kick away from him and sped toward the goal. I outmaneuvered a boy who tried to steal the ball and drove in for the goal. The goalie grabbed the ball and threw it out.

Bootblack made a goal. I took the next chance and shepherded the ball down the field. I slammed it into the goal. I doubt the boy there even saw it go by. My team cheered.

Bootblack made a long kick, and I sprang into the air and headed it back, to everyone's astonishment, including mine.

"I've never seen you play so well," Bootblack puffed to me at the next kick.

"Thank you," I said.

We played hard for an hour, as though the good name of Hungary depended on this one game. At last I managed the last goal, and ten little boys came dancing and cheering to congratulate me and themselves.

"What was that for?" Bootblack said later, as we stood by the water buckets.

"I just felt like playing."

"Warn me next time if it's going to be serious."

He grinned and hit me with the towel he had been wiping his face with.

* * *

Late in the afternoon, thunder brought Anna and Ilona to the clothesline. They snapped away the clothespins faster than birds pick up seeds. The clothes dropped into the baskets, half-folded and tidy, and just as the rain began, the girls ran in with the wash safe and dry.

After supper, Pastor Toth held the boys in their places. The rain pounded down on the roof.

"Tonight," he said, "we're going to do something different. We have someone who can play the mandolin now, so we're going to have a songfest."

He started right in with a folk song, and the boys, I was surprised to see, joined in. I could hardly hear the mandolin for the loud and hearty singing. Hymns followed the folk songs. Prayer followed the hymns.

"Good night, boys," he said. "Go straight to bed. And quietly."

I hung back, putting chairs and benches up to the tables. The Vrabel girls came and went, laying out things for morning. At last, Ilona passed near enough for me to speak to her.

"You play very well."

"Thank you. I like to play."

"I heard you last night."

"Oh, I'm sorry. I didn't think I was playing so loud. I'm sorry to have kept you awake."

"Oh, no, I liked it. You should have played longer."

She laughed a little. "Mama thought it was long enough." She looked away and then back. "How come you didn't sing tonight?"

I felt my ears burn.

"I don't sing."

"Why not?"

"I–I'm not very–musical."

"Oh."

"It doesn't matter. I'm going to be a doctor, and they don't often have to sing."

She laughed again. "I suppose not. I rather thought you would be a preacher, though."

I must have looked surprised.

"No. I've always planned to be a doctor."

She looked at me, or into me, but said nothing.

I said, "Well, I have to get to the dormitory. Good night."
"Good night."

* * *

When the conference guests gathered in the main hall, the singing vibrated the very floor. Ilona played the mandolin–at least I could see her fingers moving over the strings. I mouthed the words, in case she should look up, perhaps at me.

She did look up, I thought, and sweep her eyes over Bootblack and me, a time or two. But I did not expect much reward for being looked at, not with my face.

Each night the hall was full, and all the windows open. Pastor Toth preached first, and then some visiting pastor spoke after. I usually had to stand along the wall with other young men, or sit in the window. It was not popular, however, to block the breeze.

The walls resounded with the preaching. Toth spoke every evening on knowing God's will. At times I felt as though the wall behind me might slide back and let me drop. But I would remind myself that I already knew what I was going to do, that my course was set.

The kitchen was no place to talk. Ilona and Anna were always running. They no longer placed pitchers on the table; they just left them before us as they passed, as though the pitchers were but weights that, once shed, could not hold up the racer.

One evening after the service, I saw the lanterns of the kitchen shining on the braids. Some of the hair, worked loose in the paces of the day, floated out on the night air like rays from the sun. I watched a moment and then went round to the door.

I planned what I would say and straightened my shirt. The door was ajar, the yellow light streaming out on the rough porch. Ilona sat in a chair by the window, her head leaning on the frame, her eyes closed. I raised my hand to knock and held it there, deciding.

Her face was smooth in sleep, her hands in her lap, palms up and fingers curled, as though someone had just taken away her paring knife and the potato she was peeling. I took my hand down and backed away.

On the last day, I went around to the kitchen to say good-bye. I hoped she might be there. Anna was.

"Hello, Zoli."

"Hello."

"Are you wanting some food or a drink?"

"No thanks. I just came to say good-bye. We're leaving tomorrow."

"Yes, I know. Are you going back to the Gymnásium?"

"No, I help my father on the farm summers."

"I see."

"Tell your mother and sisters good-bye for me, if I don't see them."

"All right. Good-bye, Zoli."

The kitchen door banged behind me. I saw the bicycles under the lean-to by the pump house. I waited on the porch hoping that she might come after all.

At last, I went into the dormitory. Dani was waiting for me, sitting on my bed.

"Read the Bible to us, Zoli bacsi."

"Only if everyone is in bed and quiet."

When the scramble subsided, I chose something to read.

O give thanks unto the Lord; for he is good: because his mercy endureth for ever.
Let Israel now say, that his mercy endureth for ever.
Let the house of Aaron now say, that his mercy endureth for ever.
Let them now that fear the Lord say, that his mercy endureth for ever.
I called upon the Lord in distress: the Lord answered me, and set me in a large place.

The Lord is on my side; I will not fear: what can man do unto me?

The psalm washed over me with strength and comfort.

I shall not die, but live, and declare the works of the Lord.

I looked at the boys gazing at me and wondered fleetingly what in this reading held them so.

Thou art my God, and I will praise thee: thou art my God, I will exalt Thee.

O give thanks unto the Lord; for he is good: for his mercy endureth for ever.

"Now read us one of the stories."

"Please. Please."

"Yes, a story."

"Just one," I said. And I read the story of David and Goliath.

I blew out the lamps and left one burning low. The night was not hot, but I could not fall asleep. A long time later, I heard Bootblack come in.

"Where were you?"

"I had to talk to Pastor," he whispered.

I was comforted.

"Oh," he said, "Ilona says good-bye."

"Oh."

He got into bed and was almost immediately snoring. At least, I thought, I beat him at soccer.

Chapter Three
Full Circle

1936

"Put down your pencils, gentlemen."

Master Padanyi closed his pocket watch. Outside the underclassmen went by to their classes, in and out of the light coming through the trees.

"Leave your papers where they are, rise, and leave the room."

I stood up easily, effortlessly, as a man does who has carried something heavy and then finds himself without it. I took the room in one more time, and the master with it, his gold watchchain disappearing into the vest fob and his eyes still sizing me up, as on that first day, which now seemed part of some other lifetime, when he had rescued me from the taunts of the more polished students.

His eye met mine, and he nodded.

"Keep your shoes shined, Mr. Galambos."

"I will, sir. Thank you."

In the hall the others waited, shaking off the nerves and the energy the examinations had not used up.

"What shall we do until they post our standings?" Bootblack said.

"It's after one," I said. "Let's eat."

We ate under the Presbytery Elm, as we called it now.

"Did you hear from the University of Bratislava?" Bootblack asked.

"Not yet. But Professor Kovaly said I might not until July."

"Look," said one of the others. "Here comes Mrs. Kovaly."

We stood, wiping our mouths on the backs of our hands and straightening our shirts.

"Boys, boys," she said, "sit down. I have only come to add a little something to your picnic."

She set down a basket and lifted off the cloth.

"Ah," said Bootblack, "pies!"

"Are all the last-year students here?" she asked.

"No, ma'am," I said.

"But if we cut these pies, they will be," Bootblack said.

"Then let's cut them," she said.

Bootblack went to tell the others he could find, and they came, as he had said they would, except Hevesi, who could not be found.

"Now tell me," she said, "where you all will be going." She looked around at us licking up the last of her work, as Kovaly himself often did, as though for all our taking, there was plenty more in their storehouses.

"Well," said one fellow, "I'm going home to take over our farm." He leaned back against the tree. "And get married."

"Aho!" we said together.

"When?" Bootblack asked.

"In a week."

Mrs. Kovaly beamed at the fellow, then at us. "What about the rest of you?"

No one else seemed to have opened that door yet.

"I'm going to teach school," said Bootblack, "in my village."

"You'll make a wonderful teacher," she said.

Most of the fellows were returning to their homes to take over farms, become clerks, or run small shops. Only I and one other said we were applying to universities.

"You must write us," she said to me. "Let us know what becomes of you in that big city."

I nodded.

I found it remarkable that she looked so much like her husband, as though she were the feminine version of him. And her way of speaking was his as well. I wondered whether he had married her because she was so much like him, or whether she was so much like him because he had married her.

When she left, going down the lawn with the napkins thrown loosely into her basket and her long, old-fashioned skirt held up in one hand and her head tilted to one side, I wished suddenly that I could paint.

* * *

"Well," said Bootblack, "shall we see if the lists are up?"

We walked toward the master's part of the building. I could not get free of the impulse to view everything as the last: the last time I would walk with Bootblack to this building, the last time I would pass by these steps, the last time I would enter these doors.

A woman from Padanyi's office was just hanging the clipboard on the lobby wall as we came in.

"You go look and tell me what it says," I said.

Bootblack glanced over, as if to argue, but did not. He peered up at the list for a long time and came back.

"Not bad," he said.

"What?"

"I am seventh."

"That's good! That's good! And me?"

"I forgot to look."

"You for–"

"No," he said, laughing. "I looked. You are second."

I caught my breath, and my eyes stung. Bootblack shook my hand and thumped me soundly on the back.

"You did it, farm boy," he said. "You made it."

I went to the list myself, then, to see whose name was above mine.

It was Hevesi's.

"He can sing," said Bootblack.

"He deserves to be first. He's had as hard a road to walk as any of us, I think."

"Did you know he is going to Bratislava?"

"What?"

Bootblack smiled widely. "Wait until he finds out he hasn't quite escaped the Evangelist of Komárom."

* * *

The next day we all went out into the city, as was the custom, in black suits and bow ties and high white collars, with big black robes billowing around us. We wore hats and carried walking sticks and cheered for ourselves through the streets of Komárom.

Hevesi went first, then I, then the rest in order of their standing. Up the finest streets we paraded, like so many peacocks, shouting to everyone. Ladies came out on their porches and steps to wave at us. Men came down into the street to shake our hands.

We wove through town to the best restaurant and stopped at the door. Hevesi stamped his cane on the boards of the steps.

"The graduates are here," he said.

The owner, a big man with red cheeks and bright eyes, threw open the door.

"Come and eat with us," he said. "Today is your day."

We snaked through the restaurant, ladies stopping us to kiss us on the head and men congratulating us, until we came to the terrace. A long table was spread for us with ham and fruit and breads of every kind.

We assembled ourselves around the table. I picked up my water glass and held it out.

"To Hevesi," I said, "the first among us."

"To Hevesi," they all said and held out their glasses.

Hevesi looked at me in surprise. I put the glass to my lips and drank.

We sat and ate, and all the while we shouted down to passers-by that we were in need of congratulations, and they were quick to call them up to us.

The restaurant owner brought us a giant cake and cut it with great ceremony. Then we were as stuffed as Christmas geese and ready to walk the town again.

We wound schoolward finally and came by two o'clock to the classroom building. We gathered in no order before the speaker's platform and waited.

Padanyi came out then and made a little speech.

"This has been your boat for these few years, and I your captain. Now the world will be your boat. I hope you have learned to sail."

We cheered him when he finished, more for his finishing than for his speaking.

"Come now, gentlemen, and receive your diplomas."

Kovaly stood up beside Padanyi with the papers. Padanyi shook each man's hand and said, "God bless you." Then Kovaly gave out the diploma.

Kovaly put his hand on every shoulder before he let the fellow go by. At times he seemed about to cry, and I wondered how I could stand it if he did.

Then, before I was ready, I was before Padanyi, shaking his hand and hearing "God bless you." I stepped around him and came face to face with Kovaly.

Kovaly's hand held out my diploma. I reached slowly for it, wanting it and not wanting it, knowing all I would gain and lose by having it.

Kovaly's hand was on my shoulder, his bright eyes on mine. I saw him as I had seen him in my village one summer day, holding out a future to me then too.

"Good-bye, son."

I could not answer him for the tightness in my throat. I felt the pressure of the line behind me, but still I waited. Then I cast away my fears of what anyone might think and embraced him, my teacher, my friend, my father.

"Go with God," he said.

I went on then, without looking back, and found a solitary place.

Under the Elm, our Christian circle convened one last time and prayed, and we walked out from under the branches into our new lives.

* * *

Bootblack and I said little on the train. The old engine ran better than it had in years. Before either of us could say what we wanted to, the train was coming into Szilas. I gathered my book bag and my tie and my diploma together and sat on the edge of the seat.

Bootblack did not look up for a long time. At last he raised his head and put out his hand. I shook it once, hard, as if that one gesture could contain all that need be said.

The train slowed and stopped. I left the car, as I had so many days in the past, and stepped up on the platform. Bootblack sat by the open window, smiling sadly out. The train lurched into motion.

"Good-bye, Professor Nandor," I called as the train pulled out.

"Good-bye, Doctor Galambos," my friend called back to me.

The train was soon gone, even the smell of its smoke.

* * *

"Zoli," said Dezső, "this letter came for you."

He came running through the hay, waving an envelope. I wiped my face with my shirttail, thankful for the momentary rest.

"It looks important." He held it out to me, pleased.

"Thank you, Dezső."

The University of Bratislava, it read. I opened it and pulled out the letter.

"What does it say, Zoli?"

"It says, little brother, that I am officially a medical student at the University of Bratislava!"

"Doctor Zoli! Doctor Zoli!" Dezső shouted. He ran about in circles. Then he ran past me, back toward the house.

"Where are you going?"

"Mama said to tell her what the letter said right away," he called.

I folded the letter and stuffed it into my pocket. It had said nothing about a scholarship.

I looked across the field at Victor and Béla and Papa. The sun was going down in a blaze of orange behind them, making them more and more outlines of work. The weather would hold until the hay was in.

My mother had supper waiting for us, though it was well after dark when we came in. She poured the milk into the glasses until we had to lean forward and take the first swallows without lifting the glasses. The lamps were up hot and bright. There was an air of holiday about the kitchen.

Even Papa noticed it, for he watched her flitting from the cupboard to the table.

"Why are the lamps so high?" Béla said.

"Mama is celebrating," said Dezső.

Papa continued to stare at Mama until she looked at him.

"Well," she said, "it is not every day someone has a son accepted into a university."

Papa turned his eyes to me.

"What do you plan to use for money?" he said.

"I hope to get a scholarship."

"And if not?"

"The money will be there, if I am to go."

Papa snorted. He took a piece of sausage from the plate.

"Hope makes easy chewing," he said. He held out his fork with a bite of sausage on it, and then put it into his mouth and chewed with exaggeration.

"When do you go?" said Mama.

"October 1."

"That's plenty of time," she said.

*   *   *

I took the train to Bratislava with only the money that I had earned from Papa during the summer.

"And what when this runs out?" he had said.

"Papa," I said, "I know I am to go to Bratislava. I know that all will be well."

"What a fool you are" was his good-bye.

I felt the same fear and pleasure I had felt taking the train to Komárom when I was fourteen. But Bratislava was much farther in many ways from Szilas.

The train came at last to the station I was waiting for. It made me feel as though I was swimming in the ocean it was so large. People bumped into me as I clambered down the steps with my bags and books.

"Name," the man said to me at the university's main office.

I told him. He ran his fingers over some files in a drawer beside him and pulled one out. He pushed his little round wire glasses back up his nose.

"I see. Will you be–"

A door opened to his left. A man half-stepped through it and shot a stern look at the clerk.

"Find me another supervisor for the second floor of Blathy. Do it now."

"Yes, Mr. Stelzer."

The man pulled the door to again with a bang. The blind on the other side flapped with the sudden motion.

The clerk sighed. "I don't suppose you are looking for work."

"Well, yes, I am."

He looked up and then dropped his eyes again. "It has to be someone with experience. Experience running a dormitory."

"I helped run an orphanage dormitory before."

He cocked his head at me.

"How many children?"

"Thirty."

The clerk looked toward the door and then back at the papers in his hand.

"How old are you?"

"Twenty-one."

He leafed through the file once more.

"Wait here a moment."

He went into Mr. Stelzer's office and was soon out again.

"The job is yours."

My heart pounded in my ears.

The clerk handed me a small book. "These are the rules. You are to see to it that the men on your floor follow them."

"How many on a floor?"

"Twenty. On your floor–" He flipped open a notebook. "On your floor mostly Gymnásium students. Two other freshmen."

"Thank you."

"If there's any trouble, you will be up for replacement, understand."

"I understand."

I sat down immediately and read through the book. Curfew at nine o'clock. Rise at six. No fighting. No drinking. The list did not look imposing to me.

I unpacked my bag and made the bed. There were two black buttons by the door, one pushed in and one out. I pushed in the second, and light flashed in the room. I jumped as though someone had smacked me. I pushed the other, and the light went out. Then I went out to survey my jurisdiction.

The Gymnásium here had already opened. Many of the younger fellows were settled in, as though they had always lived there.

"Who are you?" said one. He had red hair.

"Zoltán Galambos."

"Are you the new supervisor?"

"Yes."

The boys laughed.

"Is that amusing?" I asked.

Another said, quietly, "It's not you. It's just that you're the third supervisor here in two weeks."

I felt vaguely as I had the day I passed out from fever in Kovaly's class.

"Why is that?"

"Room 210," said Red Hair.

"Room 210?"

They all nodded. But they offered no details.

At nine o'clock, Room 210 was still empty.

I wanted to know who lived there, but I did not want to ask at the office and risk losing my job the same day I had gotten it.

I went outside, hoping to find the loiterer nearby. After an hour, I went to bed with dimming hope.

In the night, someone rapped at my door.

"Come in."

A boy about fourteen leaned in.

"Mr. Galambos, you'd better come out here."

I was on my feet instantly.

"What is it?"

"A fight."

In the hall I saw nothing, heard nothing.

"Where?"

The boy motioned for me to follow him into his room. A group of boys were crowded around the window, looking down. Under the streetlight I could see two fellows about my size, rolling and punching.

I was down the stairs and into the street in seconds.

I pulled the top man off and held him back with my hand on his chest. The smell of liquor hung in the air all around him. He pushed at me, but missed. Had it not been for my hand, he would have probably fallen from the effort.

The other moaned and came to his hands and knees. He coughed and swore into the grass of the lawn.

"Who are you?" I asked.

The fellow leaning against my hand said, "Otto."

"Do you live here?"

He shook his head.

I nudged the one in the grass with my toe.

"What about you?"

He coughed again but did not answer.

I reached down and grabbed his hair. With a jerk I arched his head back into the light.

"Pali!"

Chapter Four
No Sword in Hand

I let go of his hair. He fell into the grass on his side.

Pali squinted, trying to make out my face.

"Zoli?" He started to laugh, which set him to coughing again. "What are you doing here?"

"Are you in Room 210?"

He laughed outrageously then. "You're the new supervisor, aren't you?"

I tossed my head toward the person leaning more and more on my hand.

"Who is this?"

"Nobody to worry about."

"Where have you been?"

"Well, aren't we nosy?"

I shoved the other fellow back from me.

"Go home. Leave. Don't let me see you around here again."

He swore something at me, but he stumbled away like a wobbling bear.

"Get up, Pali." I held out my hand. "You're drunk."

"No," he said, "I'm not. Last night I was."

I hauled him up and pushed him into the dormitory ahead of me. He staggered on the stairs, grabbing the rail.

"Sober, huh?" I said.

He took another two steps up and swayed backward. I took his arm around my neck and hoisted him the rest of the way.

Boys' heads stuck out of every doorway.

"To bed. Now!"

The heads disappeared, and doors snapped shut down the hallway.

I threw Pali onto his bed. He made no move to be comfortable. He just lay there like a sack of grain, his legs draping off the side. I took a pillow for myself and lay down across the doorway.

I jolted awake at a noise that sounded like someone pulling chains through a pipe. The gray light of morning showed Pali still lying where I had left him, except now he was curled up on his side.

I went out to make sure that the boys were up. The awful noise stopped at last, but my ears still rang.

"What was that?" I said to Red Hair.

"What? The bells, you mean?"

"Bells?"

He nodded and pointed to a shiny little dome about the size of a teacup on the wall.

"Downstairs is the switch. They ring us awake."

"Yes," I said, "indeed."

All but Pali, it seemed. I joggled the bed by its iron foot rail.

"Pali, wake up."

He stirred and rolled over.

"Get up," I said.

I smacked his cheek lightly. It felt hot. I shook him then until he opened his eyes.

"Pali, are you sick? Look at me, Pali."

"You again."

"Can you stand up?"

He dragged his legs off the bed and put his feet on the floor.

"You need a doctor."

He grabbed my arm with a suddenness that startled me.

"No. I'm fine. Just a cold."

He did not look at me. He let his arm drop, as though exhausted. His clothes were too big for him and reeked of sweat and beer. His hair was dirty, and he had two days' growth of beard.

"Pali." I squatted down in front of him. "What's happened to you?"

He stopped staring at the floor and stared at me. His eyes were red around the rims and dark below. It surprised me, in this morning light, that I had even recognized him the night before, that I had seen anything in this face to remind me of the cocky boy I had tutored for a year in Komárom. After several seconds, he pulled himself up straight.

"Nothing. How did you happen to come here of all places?"

"I came to study medicine. I think now the Lord sent me."

Pali coughed as though he would rip his lungs. When he stopped, he smirked at me.

"Kovaly got to you, did he?"

I stood up, pulling him with me by the collar. I held him before me, my anger coursing. His eyes went wide and then nonchalant.

"Kovaly was never anything but kind to you. You might remember that if you want to keep your teeth."

I shoved him ahead of me out the door and to the showers.

It is hard to shave someone who has two days' beard and who is unwilling.

"I'm bleeding!"

"Here." I handed him a bit of newspaper.

He clamped it to the nick on his chin.

"If you don't like the way I do it, get up and do it yourself tomorrow."

I managed to get out of him that he was in his last year of the Gymnásium, and I escorted him to class. I told the instructor, Mrs. Pikna, that I would be back after class to see him safely to the next.

That evening I sat in his room, tutoring him once again in Latin. He lounged against the bed, watching me.

"You're not listening. Get this."

"No one's paying you any more, Zoli."

"What?"

"Why are you doing this? Christian charity?"

I closed the book and got up.

"I wish I could say it was. The fact is–I want this job, and you are not going to lose it for me."

He laid his head back on the bed and smiled up at me, the same smile I remembered seeing so long ago the day I met him, the day Kovaly had told me he thought I might change Pali's record.

"Not for old time's sake, Professor?"

I sighed.

"Go to bed, Pali. You need the sleep."

* * *

My own classes started in the university. I found that I was at the bottom again, looking at upperclassmen with awe and a little envy. The buildings were immense and grand, with fine banisters on the stairs and heavy oil paintings in the entrance.

On a free hour I wandered the halls. Through an open door a rich voice came, talking of Hungarian history, enlivening a thousand years ago. I stood outside, behind the door, until change of classes.

The next day I asked the professor to let me sit in his class.

"You are not required to take history?" he said.

"No, sir. I'm a medical student. But–"

I had no means to explain that I felt bound to learn all that came within my reach or that I had listened to him teach as a child listens to a story.

"Just ambitious?" he said.

I smiled and waited.

"Sit in, then," he said. "And welcome. But the tests come with the bargain."

"Yes, sir."

I watched for Hevesi. I thought I saw him at the far end of the hall one morning, but I wasn't sure until I got to history class. There he sat, in the back. His eyes narrowed when he saw me, but he did not seem surprised.

"Hello," I said.

He tipped his head slightly, as though he had studied just how little movement he could make and still have it count as a nod.

"Quite a change from Komárom," I said.

This time his eyebrow arched up, and one side of his mouth pulled up, as if the two parts were attached, the eyebrow drawing up the corner of the lip with it.

"Quite," he said.

The anatomy professor taught in Slovak. The chemistry teacher taught in Czech. The French and English classes were partly Hungarian, partly the other languages. Sometimes at the end of the day I understood no words at all.

English was especially hard. So many words sounded the same, were spelled differently, and had three or four meanings apiece. More verbs did not follow the rules than did. I wondered how a doctor in Hungary could possibly need this language.

The English professor was waiting for his answer. It was only the second week, but already he wanted dialogue.

"I–" I sorted through the few regular verbs I knew. "I walked here."

"Very good," he said in English. "What do you study?"

"I study–" The words for *medicine* and *surgery* retreated. "I study–books."

A few laughs rippled through the class. I held my breath. The professor surveyed my face.

"Cunning," he said in Hungarian.

I looked down at my book, at the pencil in my hand.

"But there will come a day," he said, "when cunning will not pass for knowledge."

* * *

"What are you doing, Mr. Galambos?"

It was Red Hair and two of his cronies.

"Reading the Bible."

"For a class?"

"No, because I want to."

Red Hair drew his head back a little and smiled like a fox.

"Why?"

"It helps me."

"I've never seen anybody read the Bible outside church before."

I went on reading.

"I'd read it to you, but I'm not sure you could understand it."

"I could understand it," said Red.

"I don't know." I shook my head, looking up at them. "Some of it's pretty hard."

"Try us," said one of the other boys.

"Well–"

"Come on. Please."

"All right."

They sat down, and I gave them David and Goliath, for I remembered that it had been a favorite at the orphanage.

Their eyes never left me.

So David prevailed over the Philistine with a sling and with a stone, and smote the Philistine, and slew him; but there was no sword in the hand of David.

A silence lasted for some seconds.

"What else is in there?" asked Red.

* * *

It was after midnight, and still no Pali. I waited in his room for him. When he switched on the light, I was sitting on a chair by the door.

"Where were you? Off with Otto drinking again?"

"Zoltán, just run your dormitory. I'll run my own life, thank you."

He brushed past me. His cheeks were red and his eyes dull.

"I think you have pneumonia," I said.

"A doctor after only two weeks."

He sat down on the bed. He tried to hold in a cough that rattled in his chest. I waited until he looked at me.

"Where do you think these choices will come out that you're making?"

He snorted at me.

"What do you care? What do I care for that matter?"

I suddenly wanted to take the chair I was sitting in and break it over his head.

"You really are an idiot, aren't you?"

Pali's eyes narrowed the tiniest bit.

"What do you want, Pali? You have the brains. Your father gives you all the money you need, you—"

"Shut up!"

"No–you shut up. It makes me sick the way you drink and gamble away money."

I was on my feet now.

"Think about it, little boy. You throw away more than most people ever have!"

Pali's eyes were hard.

"You want money? I'll have my father hire you again. I'm sure that will make you both happy."

"You think money will fix everything, don't you?"

Pali did not move or change his expression.

"I'm not the one who thinks that. I've never been the one who thinks that."

"Meaning what?"

He shoved back and leaned up against the iron rails of the bed.

"Don't talk about things you don't understand, Zoli. It makes you look ridiculous."

"And how is it you are so wise, you with such a hard life?"

He sat forward, pointing a finger at me like an angry school teacher.

"I'm warning you, Zoltán. Stay out of my business."

I scraped the chair back to its place by the dresser.

"Then stay out of mine. Make curfew from now on."

* * *

Two days later Pali was too weak to get out of bed. The doctor ordered him to the hospital. Pneumonia, he said.

I walked to the hospital with some of Pali's books. The air was cold; but I liked autumn cold–it was never as chilly as spring's. Bratislava was a huge place. I had not imagined that the hospital would be miles from the university.

The woman in the entrance wore a white headdress that was folded into a sort of box around her face and hung down straight in the back. I could not decide whether she was a nun or a nurse.

"No visitors but family, sir," she said. "I'm sorry."

"Well, could you tell him Zoltán Galambos was here? And give him these?"

I held out the books.

"What's this?" a woman's voice behind me said. "Cousin Zoli? Is it really you?"

I turned and was enveloped in an embrace and a cloud of perfume. I drew back quickly. A girl my own age with short blonde hair was smiling at me, at the nurse, at the world.

"How good of you to come, dear Zoli." She looked past me to the nurse. "It's all right. This is Pali's favorite cousin. All the way from Budapest."

She took my arm and steered me away with her. I glanced back at the nurse who did not look convinced but who was not following us.

The girl pulled me into the stairway.

"Come on, cousin." She laughed a bubbling laugh.

"Who–"

"I'm Milike, Pali's sister. Pali said you might be coming. Did you see her face?" She laughed again. She stepped back and looked at me. "You don't look a bit like any of us. Maybe Hugo bacsi."

I was smiling at her, despite myself.

"Let's go," she said. "Pali's waiting."

She took my hand and led me up.

Pali lay still, white on white pillows. His bed was near the one window in the long room. The light coming in seemed to diffuse in the hospital air, giving the whole place a hazy appearance. Pali barely smiled when we came in.

"So you were right, doctor," he said, hardly a whisper.

"I'm sorry I was."

He shook his head a little bit, as though the things of two days ago were but trivial now.

Milike took the books and put them on the floor by the bed. She was down and up again like a sparrow.

"Pali's not supposed to talk," she said. "That's why I came." She spoke softly now, not at all as she had downstairs. "Papa always said I was the one destined for politics."

"Is there anything else he needs?" I said.

"I don't think so," she said. "Just rest and medicine–and me."

Pali closed his eyes.

She mouthed to me "Let's go out" and motioned to the hall.

She went out ahead of me and chose a bench under a tall window at the end of the hall.

"Thank you for coming down. Pali used to talk about you all the time."

"I never saw you at the house."

"No, I was in a girls' school," she said. "I came home only once or twice a month, on weekends."

The sun shone across her hand. I wanted to touch it again.

She said, "You study medicine now?"

"Yes."

"That's good." She glanced away. "I wanted to go to the university once. But I have a job in the city now."

"Here? In Bratislava?"

She looked at me again.

"Yes. Pali didn't tell you?"

I shook my head. I did not tell her that Pali had never even mentioned that he had a sister.

"You came from Szilas, don't I remember? What does your father do?"

"He farms."

For the first time since we had sat down, I looked away from her. She seemed like sunlight itself, there on the bench beside me. And I felt suddenly like a cloud, weighted with rain and darkness. I moved away from her a little and crossed my ankle over my knee.

"Pali will be all right," I said. "It's good he's here finally. I tried to make him come before."

"Pali's stubborn sometimes."

We sat without speaking for a minute or more.

"Milike, I would be glad to–"

She tipped her head, waiting for me to finish.

"That is, would you like me to walk you home?"

"Well, I'm not leaving right away."

"I can come back," I said. "It's not far."

* * *

Pali was in the hospital six days. I went every day after classes to see whether he would be getting out. Three times Milike was there, and three times I walked her home. The day Pali came back to the dormitory, she came with him.

"You'll have to wait in the lobby," I said. "That's the rule."

"You are one for rules, aren't you? Very well, I'll be here."

Pali kissed her on the cheek.

"Thanks," he said.

She patted his face.

I carried his books and the new clothes Milike had given him to his room.

"Do you want to eat something?" I said.

"No, I think I'll sleep."

He studied me as though we had only just met. He raised his eyes to mine in a knowing look. I knew a warning when I saw one.

"See you later." My hand was on the door.

Pali sat down on the bed without seeming to notice when I left.

"I have to get to English class," I said to Milike.

"Oh, English!" she said. "Do you think you could teach me? I am going to travel one of these days–and America is the first place I want to go."

"Why there?"

"Because America is still new. It's not all tramped over yet, and dingy, and tired."

I laughed at her, at her talk that was ever coming to the surface like spring water.

She took my hand and held it to her cheek.

* * *

The snow finally came, whipping over the sidewalks and between the buildings. It howled outside, as though it resented being kept from classes.

"The wind's bad tonight," said Red Hair. He sat in the hall just outside my door.

"Do you think?"

He nodded. "Some of us were wondering–"

"Yes?"

"If you are going to throw Pali out."

"What?"

"You know," he said. "From school."

"That's not for me to do," I said.

I went into my room. Red Hair followed.

"Hey–" I said.

"Don't you like Pali?"

"Did I ask you in here?"

He backed out of the door, but he didn't leave.

"I was just wondering. You're always yelling at him."

I put my books on the dresser and caught sight of myself in the small mirror.

"Of course I like him. Now go on."

I wandered around the room, thumbing through books and putting them down, polishing my shoes, staring out the window at the snow. I tried to read the Bible, but the words clattered against my mind like beads of snow on the glass.

A long while later, I heard Pali come in. I went and stood outside his door and finally knocked.

"Yeah."

He saw who it was and went on pulling off his shoes. I stood in the doorway, waiting.

"Well?" he said.

I stepped farther in. From my pocket I took a letter, still unsealed.

"I wrote your father."

"About dating Milike, I suppose?"

I hesitated. "About you."

Pali was on his feet, his eyes snapping. He snatched the paper.

"I warned you!"

His fists trembled at his side, and the veins on his neck stood out. He glared at me as though I had threatened to take his best possession. I held up my hand.

"What is—"

He lunged forward and took a swing at me. I stepped back out of his reach. He came at me again, but I grabbed his arm and brought him down to his knees. He wrenched his wrist free, swearing at me, and then he thrust his whole body into my chest.

I sprawled backward and was up in the same instant, driving into him. I shoved him backward and pinned him to the floor. I crouched above him like a panther. His eyes looked wild.

"What?" I demanded. "What?"

He struggled against my hold, jamming my ribs with his knee. I took hold of his chin from underneath and pushed his head down.

"Stop it, Pali. I can hurt you."

His eyes went dim, like a lamp turned down, and the fingers boring into my forearm relaxed. He turned his head and squinted his eyes shut; his mouth drew back as if he were in pain. Thus we lay for seconds together, until he gasped in some air and let it out in a shuddering sob.

I let go of him and got up and away, quiet as a shadow. He turned on his side and covered his face. The sobs shook his whole body, as though he were sucking in stones with his gasps.

I sat against the overturned chair watching him, feeling an ache in my chest that could not be totally accounted for by the blow he had delivered in the fight. I waited a long time.

"I'm sorry, Pali."

He sighed as a man might who looks out at the ruin of his farm.

"What are you sorry for?"

After another moment he hoisted himself to a sitting position. He reached for the dresser drawer and with some effort pulled it open. He felt under the clothes there and pulled out something wrapped in a shirt. Looking at me, he lifted the cloth up. Out onto the floor fell a pistol.

I looked at it and up to Pali again. His face was the face of a man who is sentenced to die.

"I sold my clothes to buy this."

I could say nothing, do nothing. The tears ran out of his eyes, but I could not look away. He took a jerking breath.

"I owe money. A lot of money. To Otto and others."

A bloated face under the street lamps and a body leaning against my hand came vaguely to me, as though through fog.

"Before you came here, I planned to kill Otto. Then–"

He raised his eyes to mine. My heart thudded under my ribs.

"I decided to kill myself."

My heart seized up. I felt as though I couldn't breathe.

"Oh, Pali."

"There's no other way out for me, Zoli. I'm done."

My hands were shaking and cold. I felt my blood roaring in my ears. The electric light seemed too bright to think under. My voice came out in a whisper.

"Nothing is ever that ruined."

"You don't know."

There was a hardness in his look that made me feel awkward and stupid.

"I know God can forgive anything."

"I'm in too deep, Zoli."

He did not change his expression. I drew a long breath.

"I know what you think of Kovaly, but I can tell you–everything he told us is true. I know it for myself."

Pali continued to look at me, but the despair was showing through.

I said, "I should have told you before." The blood pounded in my temples. "Can I tell you now?"

He sat, his hands beside him, palms up, as though he had not the strength to lift them. His look made me feel I should cover my face.

"Please listen to me."

He nodded, once, quickly, the smallest nod.

"Wait right here. Will you? You'll wait one second?"

I held his gaze until I was sure. Then I picked up the pistol.

"I'll make you a trade, Pali. A Bible for this."

Chapter Five

Horsemen

The snow had packed down under hundreds of footsteps into a slick glaze. I decided to walk in the loose snow and get wet rather than try to keep my balance on the ice.

Ahead, a woman seemed to be coming to speak to me. She came straight toward me, but I did not recognize her.

"Mr. Galambos?"

"Yes?"

She held out her hand, and I took it.

"I'm Professor Pikna, from the Gymnásium. Pali's Latin teacher."

"Oh, yes. It's been a while. I'm sorry I didn't–"

"Not at all. I've been hoping to see you sometime."

"Yes?"

"You're Pali's tutor, aren't you?"

"Yes, his father hired me early this year."

"I cannot tell you what a change you've worked in Pali. I am indeed grateful. And I don't just mean in Latin."

"I'm afraid I can't claim–"

"Tut, tut, Mr. Galambos. You may not know what he was like before you came."

I smiled.

"But," she went on, "I am not the only one to have noticed the difference."

"Have you asked Pali about his new self?"

"Well, no. To be honest, I was afraid that might break the spell."

"Ask him, Professor. I am sure you won't change him in the least."

She looked at me a little askance.

"Perhaps I shall. It must be quite the story."

"Indeed it is."

She dipped her head gracefully to me and passed on by. I felt like singing, and being alone on the sidewalk, I did.

Pali was in my room, his books spread out under the window. Red Hair was there, too, leaning against my bed, tossing a ball from one hand to the other.

"Since when did you fellows move in here?"

"Ah," said Red Hair, "we like it in here, Mr. Galambos."

"Yeah, Mr. Galambos," said Pali. He grinned.

"Does anyone mind if I use the desk?" I said.

"No," said Pali, "go ahead."

Red Hair nodded agreement.

"Thank you," I said.

"Mr. Galambos?"

I looked over at the boy. He still passed the ball back and forth.

"I can't listen to you or Pali read the Bible any more. Papa doesn't like it."

I glanced at Pali.

"I'm sorry," I said.

Red Hair held the ball still, as though he might study it.

"And–"

We waited.

"And he might come down here and make you not read it at all."

I opened my French book and said nothing more.

In a while Red Hair went to find livelier company. I pulled out an envelope with money in it and handed it to Pali.

He took it slowly, his eyes down.

"Thanks."

"Thanks to your father," I said.

There was a change in the room, as when a cloud passes over the sun and the light diminishes.

"Mrs. Pikna stopped me today. She can't get over how you've changed."

"I suppose not."

I turned the pages of my book as though I were looking for something.

Pali said without looking up, "I'll pay this all back, Zoli."

"I know."

"I mean it." He finally raised his eyes.

"It's all right. I told you."

He put the envelope in his history book. I wondered how much he still owed, but I never asked.

* * *

"It's soon Christmas," Milike said.

Always when we walked together, she seemed to take twice as long a walk as I, for she would step fast to get slightly ahead and look at me squarely when she asked a question. Or she would turn out to the side to dust snow from the evergreen branches and come back, like a snowbird, still chirping.

I nodded and looked at her out of the corner of my eye.

"Are you going home to Szilas?" she said.

She skipped out in front of me and walked backwards, watching my face.

"I hadn't decided."

"Well, I was thinking—you could come with Pali and me to Budapest. We have Christmas at the winter house there."

She fell back into step beside me and took my arm.

"Want to?"

"I'll have to see," I said.

We came to the end of the sidewalk. A carriage sat there, its driver dozing under a blanket and the horse pawing the hard snow. Milike went up and patted the horse on the neck. The animal threw its head around to nip at her. She deftly lifted her arm up and away.

"Whoa," she said. "What's this?"

She went to stand before the horse. She stroked its nose, several light taps. It tossed its head again, but not as hard.

"Come on, be nice," she said.

The horse stood quiet then, breathing out gusts of frost.

"We have riding horses, Zoli, in Budapest. Do you like to ride?"

"Yes."

I did not tell her that my sole mount had been a plow horse, when Papa had put me up to drive between the rows of corn when we cultivated, and that I could never stand up straight at the end of such riding.

"See what fun we could have?" she said. "Pali rides very well. At least he used to."

"It's going to snow again," I said. "Perhaps we should start back."

She came without arguing and took my arm again.

"I've asked Papa, if that's what's bothering you."

"Oh," I said. "There are several things I have to think about."

In a little while, large wet flakes began to fall. The top of her scarf and her shoulders were soon covered. I brushed off her scarf.

"No, leave it. Let's see how deep it gets."

"You'll get wet," I said.

"You are one to worry, aren't you?"

*   *   *

History class seemed to hold the students' attention more than any other class I was in. It was Professor Fenyo's style, surely, for I could not explain my sudden thirst for history by any other means.

"Hungarian Premier Teleki once said that Hungary had a Parliament before it had chairs."

The professor paced the center aisle of his classroom. He made me think that he was better suited to military action than to academics.

"And what do you think the Premier meant?"

No one spoke. The professor continued pacing. He often made two or three trips up and down without repeating his question. His pacing and his silence often drove us to the answers.

Someone in the front row said, "He meant that when Chieftain Árpád held the first Hungarian Assembly he did so on horseback. In 902 the great horsemen had no buildings yet from which to govern their new nation."

The professor stopped and regarded the student. "How new?"

"Six years, sir. Hungary began in 896."

"Yes. All right, that's the literal meaning. However, I don't think Regent Horthy would applaud a simple history lesson from Mr. Teleki. What did the Premier imply?"

Again there was silence. At last, the teacher looked at me.

"What do you think he meant, Mr. Galambos?"

I took a long breath. "That Hungary is inherently democratic?"

He almost smiled. "Explain yourself."

My heart beat faster; I could feel the color rising in my cheeks.

"He may have meant that because Hungary had the spirit of rule by the people before she had anything else, she should not forget democracy easily."

"Very good." He walked past. "Very good."

I caught Hevesi staring at me. Our eyes met; he did not look away. I felt my brows draw together, a silent question to Hevesi. He gave no response. Slowly, without turning his head, he took his eyes from me and looked back to the teacher.

The teacher stood at the front now.

"I think sometimes that you students don't connect what you learn in history to anything that's happening around you. I am not teaching in a vacuum, I hope."

He picked up a newspaper.

"Do any of you read the papers?"

A few students raised their hands. I thought of Bootblack; he always seemed to know what the papers had said.

"Does anyone know what's going on in Spain?"

"There's a civil war there, sir," someone said.

"Yes. But what is going on?"

We all looked at him as though surely he would realize that he had repeated himself.

He stared out at us as he might at urchins. Then he laid down the paper and folded his arms.

"Follow me now," he said. "Who rules Germany?"

"Adolph Hitler," we said.

"And who rules Italy?"

"Mussolini," the man beside me said.

"Does anyone know what they have to do with the Spanish Civil War?"

There was a pause, this time with no good effect.

The professor said, "Hitler is sending guns; Mussolini is sending men. They want to help overthrow the existing government in Spain. Are you with me?"

"Yes, sir."

"Can anyone tell me what Hitler tried to do two years ago in Austria?"

"Yes!" The speaker was a young woman who had never before said anything in class as far as I knew. "He tried to take it over."

"Correct," he said. "Tried, but failed. Now then, think. What reasons might Hitler have for sending war equipment to Spain?"

The man beside me spoke again. "Could he be trying to gain an ally?"

"Who?"

"Spain?"

"And?"

I said, "Mussolini?"

"Yes, Italy. Why?"

I shook my head. I hoped he would not call my name again.

"What would Hitler gain by making Mussolini an ally?"

A man behind me said, "A Marxist friend."

"Precisely. Now if the Spanish government falls, the victors will set up a Marxist government. Then there will be three."

I thought how little thinking I really did.

"But," he went on, "Hitler may be doing something else by helping Spain."

He waited. Perhaps a whole minute passed.

The girl spoke again, at last, tentatively, hardly a whisper.

"Maybe he's trying to look like a power to reckon with."

Several of us turned to look at her.

"You may be quite right," said the teacher. "And so in the future Austria may face a greater foe. A foe with friends this time. And does anyone know where Hitler sent troops last March?"

No one seemed to.

"Into the Rhineland. And there was no response from France at all. What does that tell you?"

At last the girl said, "That he already is a power to reckon with."

"Perhaps," he said.

Then he stood straight, and the former pensiveness almost visibly dropped from him. He smiled at us, one of his rare smiles.

"Now stay with me just a bit longer. What good does studying history do you then?"

There was shocked silence all around. We had never thought a teacher might perceive prejudices against studies. He waited again, without pacing, to let the question settle on us.

"Well," he said, "suppose someone did not know how long a history his country has. Would he stand as long in its defense as a man who knew what greatness came before him?"

We shook our heads.

"And if you can see where choices have led out in the past, you may learn to make better choices in the future?"

"Yes, sir," several of us said.

"So you do well to study Árpád and his horsemen?"

We did not answer the question because it was not a question.

"You could say that the history of Hungary is hoofprints in the snow. And Hungarians would do well to mind where they have ridden from and where they are riding to now."

It came to me, like a voice from another room, the chant of my childhood–no, no, never! Never would we surrender our Hungarian heritage.

* * *

I found Pali sitting in his room, well into the dusk, with no light on. I went in without asking, without even speaking. Two steps into the room, I could smell the liquor.

"What have you done?"

There was no answer. He faced out the window, as though he were a statue someone had put there to represent isolation.

"Pali."

"Please leave me alone."

"You know better than this."

"Don't preach at me." Still he had not moved.

"What happened?"

There was a threat in his silence.

I sat down on the end of the bed. The springs squeaked. For some time I just sat there, until his silhouette blended more and more with the shadows outside.

"What happened?" I asked again.

He leaned forward into the panes. He put his elbow on the sill and held his forehead with his hand.

"I'm asking you, Zoli. Leave me alone. I'll be all right."

"I don't think so."

He pushed away from the window and spoke into the dark.

"Report me, Zoltán. Write my father. Do what you want. Just get out."

I stood up.

"You don't know what you're doing."

"I think I do."

I left, slamming the door behind me.

In the morning Pali was up and gone before the bells. I could not go look for him; there was so much else to be done. At noon I walked to the Gymnásium.

"Mrs. Pikna, excuse me. Have you seen Pali?"

"Yes, he was in class this morning. Is something wrong?"

"No," I said, stepping back. "I was just wanting to see him."

I wandered away to my own classes with a heavy feeling that was not entirely worry for Pali. I felt uneasy, but I could not name the cause.

After supper some younger boys came to hear about Samson. At the end Pali came in and sat among the listeners. When I finished, I said I needed to study, and they all left. Pali stayed.

We sat without speaking. I opened my English book and took out a copybook.

"About last night," he said.

I looked up.

"I'm sorry."

I still said nothing.

"Just–"

"Just what?" I said.

"Just, well, just don't always think you have to–to ride in on every battle."

I felt my jaw tighten.

"I am in charge here," I said.

Pali sighed and stood up.

"Do what you have to, Zoli. Just don't be so condescending."

* * *

It got warmer for a few days. By the time most of the snow had melted, so had Pali's aloofness. We walked through new snow to check our mail. There were two folded papers for me, standing at a slant in the box.

I unfolded one, a grade card. I had a B- in French, a B in chemistry, a B in biology, a B in anatomy, and a C in English. Fenyo had not recorded a grade for history.

Pali had a B in Latin.

"That's a sight I've never seen," Pali said. "So that's what a B looks like." He turned to me. "Look at your grades, Zoli. All lined up there like pretty girls."

I looked, but I could not shake the disappointment.

"And a letter, too," said Pali.

I unfolded the other paper that had been in my box.

"Zoli, Milike told me she asked you for Christmas. Do you know if you–what?"

I held out the paper I had been reading for him to read.

He scanned it and looked up, alarmed.

I read it again myself and folded it back up.

"You think Red's father got to Stelzer?" Pali said.

"What else could it be?"

I pulled my cap on again.

I quoted, "You are a supervisor in our employ. You are not to use your position to spread your personal opinions."

We walked back another way, making the first tracks in the snow on that side of the building.

"Well," said Pali, "I'm not employed here."

"Yes, but that's not the real issue."

"Yes, it is. I'll read to the boys, and things will be the same."

"No, they won't. Not for me."

There seemed nothing more to be said. Pali swiped snow from the low wall beside us.

"What is this with the snow," I said, "a family trait?"

"What?"

"Hitting the snow off things. Milike does it all the time."

"Oh." Pali laughed. "Maybe. So–are you coming for Christmas?"

I pulled the end of my scarf until the wool tightened around my neck.

"Do you think you could teach me to ride a horse? I mean properly ride a horse?"

Pali smiled sideways at me. "Of course."

We came to the dormitory and stomped our feet. Pali put his hand on my shoulder and leaned in as if to tell a secret.

"Milike always sleeps late on holiday," said he. "We could ride early." He winked. "I like it better then anyway."

* * *

When the train pulled into Budapest, evening and snow were coming down together. The streetlamps seemed like balls of light hanging in the air over the sidewalks.

"There's so much to see," said Milike, "as soon as the snow lets up."

We took a carriage to their house, although motorcars were also waiting at the station for riders.

"The house is on the west side," said Pali. "You can't see the Danube from there though."

The horses' hooves thudded softly, and the harness jingled. I leaned forward to watch the city pass by.

"Do you like museums, Zoli?" Milike asked.

"Yes." At least I thought I would.

"Then we'll go to the National one day."

I could feel the weight of her cape on my knee. When we passed under a lamp, I caught a glimpse of her face and hair. She seemed already quieter, more at ease, as though breathing the Budapest air were restoring a spirit straitened by Bratislava.

The carriage rolled up before a stone house, every window of which held a candle. The lamps on the either side of the door, I could tell, were electric.

Pali and I pulled down the luggage. The driver leaned out from his perch only to take money from Pali.

"Don't say too much about the house," Pali said. "It was in our mother's family. Papa keeps it only because Milike loves it here."

The entryway was bright, candles and lamps burning generously. A fire leaped up the chimney in the room off the entry.

"Well, here we are," said Milike. "But where is Papa?"

"Here, child."

Then he was there, a small man with a small mustache, coming toward us from the other end of the entry hall. Milike flew to him and kissed him many times on both cheeks. When she stepped back, laughing, he cocked a glance up at me.

"Here is Zoli," she said. She took his hand and brought him forward.

He held out his hand, and I took it.

"I'm pleased to see you, sir."

"And you." He turned to Pali. "Hello, son."

"Father."

To me he said, "So this is your first time in Budapest?"

"Well, no, sir, I was here once, as a child–"

"Papa," said Milike, "here we all stand in the hall and such a wonderful fire burning. Come, let's go in. Shall I get us some tea or something?"

She linked her arm in his, and we all followed her, drawn, I suspect, as much by her warmth as the fire's.

* * *

"Come on." It was Pali's voice.

"What?"

"Come. Get up. I'll have the horses saddled by the time you're dressed. Just come out the front. Be quiet, though."

It was early, but the air was already bright. The snow lay full and sparkling down the steps and flowed uninterrupted to the street. Pali was waiting, sitting on a black horse, holding the reins of a gray. When I came out, he got down.

"This is how you mount," he said.

He stood on the left of the horse, the reins draped loosely in his right hand. He lifted his left foot to the stirrup. He pushed off with his right leg and swung it up and over.

"Now, here's your horse, Gyöngy–the Pearl." He leaned forward and handed me the reins.

I held my right hand at the front of the saddle and put my left foot in the stirrup. Gyöngy moved right. I hopped along. Pali nudged his horse alongside mine.

"Now try it."

I managed to get in the saddle.

"The rest is easy," Pali said.

We rode for some time, and it did become easier, but I could not quite get the knack of keeping a good seat, though, as Pali called it. I bounced more than was meet, and I felt all loose in my joints.

We stopped and dismounted somewhere. I had completely lost direction, being so concerned with my horsemanship.

"I haven't ridden in a long time," Pali said.

"Why?"

He shrugged.

"I don't think of it when I'm away. And I haven't been here in three years."

The long morning shadows reached toward us. Pali's horse bobbed its head and snorted. Pali took a little tighter grip up the reins.

"I thought I should come this year. To try to fix things."

He glanced up.

"My father and I–"

"You don't have to explain."

"My father and I have had many differences."

"Won't that change now? I mean, since you've–"

Pali looked steadily at me with that look he sometimes had that made me feel very, very young, and I dwindled off.

"It's not so simple, you know, to change what has been built year by year."

I straightened the twist out of a rein.

Pali said, "I used to feel he loved Milike more." He tapped one boot against the other and smiled, still looking at his feet. "But she is lovable, isn't she?"

I stood there in the snow without an answer.

"When I was little, I used to pretend that I didn't have a sister. I thought that he would like me more if I didn't have a sister."

Still I found I had nothing to say.

"But it wasn't Milike. It was me."

I looked away, back the way we had come. The two lines of prints seemed to weave in and out from each other and finally come together at a distant point.

"Do you think things are ever beyond fixing?"

"I'm not sure," I said. "Maybe it depends on what is past."

The bells of a church rang somewhere. For some reason they made me think of Szilas and the morning the bells had rung and the teacher had cried, standing among the scattered pieces of the map. And in that moment, I felt lonely.

Pali's horse snorted again, and Pali seemed to recover himself.

"Well, enough of this," he said. "Let's ride back."

I put my foot in the stirrup, and the horse shifted sideways. Again I tried; this time my shoe slipped out of the stirrup. The third time I got up. I cast a glance at Pali's boots. It occurred to me that I might be able to ride better if I had the right clothes.

Chapter Six
Heroes Before

Chieftain Árpád still sat astride his great horse in Heroes' Square. I stood before him, his bronze self gleaming with boldness and past victory. The plume of his helmet pointed skyward, and his jaw seemed set, not by molder's art, but by a fierce determination to be always looking ahead and to pass that vision to the future.

The plaque said the statue had been put up in 1896, when Hungary was one thousand years old. The afternoon sun threw the Chieftain's shadow behind him, and I took courage, believing there was safety in a shadow more than a thousand years long.

Milike had to pull me away from Heroes' Square, from Árpád's noble gaze outward, back down the broad avenue. We passed the Opera House.

"I went to an opera there once," she said. "It was so lovely."

But I was thinking of the statues, of the horses forever standing in their bronze trappings, their necks arched against the rule of the masterful hands that held the reins. How superb to be born a Hungarian, I thought, to descend from such strength.

"Have you ever seen an opera?"

"What? Oh, no, I haven't."

Motorcars roared past, and wind gusted against us.

"I don't think I should like to," I said.

The day was bright and warm for December. I wanted to walk the whole city.

"I wish I could find the place where my father stood that morning I saw Horthy ride across the bridge."

"Which bridge was it?"

"I don't know–I was so little, you know. I didn't even know what city my memory held until I was in school and the teacher talked about Horthy's ride into Budapest."

"Maybe Papa knows which bridge. We'll ask him."

The reality of the buildings and bridges around me nearly erased the filmy recollections I had of the white horse.

"Are you having a good time, Zoli?"

"I can't remember a better time."

As soon as I said it, I felt a tug at the inside of my heart. The days I had spent at Kovaly's house getting well came up before me, and I felt oddly as though I had betrayed someone.

Budapest seemed half-populated with statues, bronze and stone, all solemn, all grand. We stopped and sat a while near Liberty Square. I thought that were I a sculptor, I should make a statue of Milike, except stone and bronze could hardly be made to hold the airy likeness.

"See that statue there?" Milike pointed across the plaza.

A man in riding boots, holding a riding crop behind him, gazed out forever with an air of command over Liberty Square.

"That's the newest. That went up last August."

"Who is it?"

"An American general. I forget his name."

"American?"

I went to see how this foreigner came to be cast forever in the capital of Hungary. The pedestal read:

HARRY HILL BANDHOLZ
In glorious memory of the heroic American general,
noble champion of justice,
the grateful Hungarian nation.

"What did he do?"

"He kept the Rumanians from taking everything out of Hungary at the end of the Great War."

"Was an American ruler of Hungary then, I wonder?"

"Just a protector. I think I remember Papa saying he saw this man. He left the day before Horthy came. The statue is here because he swooped in on the Rumanian army with his riding whip and stopped them from destroying the National Museum."

I studied the face again. It seemed a good face to me.

"Look at these," Milike said.

She took my hand and pulled me along, as children do when they feel they have been patient long enough.

We came to a statue of a man and a woman, the man's shield half-covering the woman, but both with defiance in the angle of their chins and the power of their gazes.

"The Statue of the South," Milike said. "It is the most lovely of all the statues, I think. Look how he protects her."

"Look how she seems not to need it," I said.

"There are the others–North, East, and West," she said.

The figures were all caught forever in the agony of death, their limbs twisted, their heads thrown back.

"What do they mean?" I said. I could not draw my eyes away.

"They stand for the lands we have lost."

"Trianon," I said. "The Treaty of Trianon."

I looked back to the South monument, and for a moment resisted the urge to put my arm around Milike. She smiled up at me, as though my idea were printed on my brow.

"Let's eat in a restaurant," said Milike. "Just a little something, shall we?"

When we found a place to eat and walked in, two young men looked up at Milike and then at me. I pulled my shoulders back and moved her hand into the crook of my arm. Milike glanced up at me, tilting her head a little. I patted her hand and surveyed the restaurant for a place to sit.

We had a piece of dark, sticky cake and coffee. I occasionally looked over to see that I was still being envied by the two at the window table.

"Papa is preaching on Christmas Day," Milike said.

"Good," I said.

"Are you in the Reformed Church?"

"No, not exactly."

"Well, it doesn't matter. As long as you're not a Catholic."

"I'm no Catholic. I'm a Christian."

Milike laughed. "Well, of course you are, silly."

I did not understand the conversation any more.

*   *   *

The horses tossed up the snow with their drumming hooves. The rocking canter was far easier to hold a seat with than the trot, I found. The drumming and the snorting of the horses were as fine a music as I could ever want.

In a few hundred yards, Pali drew up his black. I slowed my horse as well and pulled it around to face Pali. Pali was breathing hard and smiling.

"How did you know how to get a canter?"

"I watched you the other day," I said.

"Good watching, I must say. It's a subtle thing. Or it's supposed to be."

"Learning by watching is a thing my father made me know."

Pali nudged his horse into a walk, and I joined him.

"So you do have a father then?" Pali said.

"What?"

"In all the years I've known you, you've never said anything about your family."

"You never mentioned Milike."

"Touché. Watch how you hold your feet, Zoli."

I pushed my heels down.

"Zoli–"

I looked over at Pali. His eyes were direct, but his mouth had the slightest upturn at the corners.

"Are you thinking of marrying Milike?"

I looked away. "No! I mean–I, well, I haven't thought that far."

"I don't think Father will allow it until you're out of school. I just thought I'd tell you that."

There was at once comfort and pain in this news. Pali turned his horse left, and I followed the lead.

I said, "Milike told me once that she had wanted to go to the university. Why doesn't she?"

Pali rode a while without speaking.

"That's hard to answer. Partly, Father doesn't believe a woman needs that much schooling."

"Well, no. But if she wants to–"

"And partly, I think he wants to keep her a little girl."

"But she works–in Bratislava."

"Yes, but that is nothing. She wanted to come where I was. I suppose Father thought she could keep an eye on me, so he let her come. And he sends her money. She couldn't live on what she makes–at least not the way she's used to."

*   *   *

The church organ vibrated the seats under us. The pipes of it shone under the arches of wood and gold like so many brass gun barrels. And every pipe had a small frown cut in it somewhere to let the vibrations out.

When Milike's father stood to speak, he was almost lost behind the richly carved pulpit, in the echoing chasm of the church. He wore a robe, but somehow it only made him look smaller.

"We come today to worship the God of Christmas," he said. His voice did not sound as it did at the house. It was deeper, and he drew his words out more.

"The God of love and peace."

His sentences rose and fell, rose and fell, until I felt vaguely as though I were on a boat. I remembered Toth's preaching, its volume and its little thrusts at my heart. I remembered how I had to stand up before, and I was glad for this more comfortable pew.

"Ever do we stray from the light of His love, ever do we wander in the darkness, when we fail to think of others."

I looked at Milike beside me, her hands in her lap, her face up to her father's words. I wished I had more to give her than the wool gloves I had bought.

The organ played again after a long while, and we all stood. Milike took my arm and Pali's, walking between us to the doors, to the street, to the house.

We ate pork and chicken and seven kinds of vegetables and bread and cake. Never had I seen a table so burdened with food.

"Did you do all this?" I asked Milike.

She laughed. "Goodness, no. We have a cook." She winked at Pali. "For which we are all grateful. There—I saved you the trouble."

He grinned at her.

"Pali used to have to eat what I cooked when we were younger. He considers it a miracle that he survived to adulthood."

She laughed, and Pali laughed. I smiled, more at their laughing than at the joke, for I had never tasted any of her cooking.

The Christmas tree in the drawing room was hung with red and silver ornaments shaped like tears. The light from the fireplace glittered on the tree, changing the way the shadows of the tree wrinkled on the wall. I caught my reflection in one of the ornaments. It exaggerated my jaw, and I stepped back, putting my hand to my chin, to be sure.

We sat for a while without speaking, any of us, and listened to the fire hissing and snapping.

"Must be the wood's a little wet," I said.

"What? Oh, yes, perhaps," said Milike's father.

"Shall we open the gifts?" Milike said. It could not have been meant as a question, for she was up before I could answer. Milike gave me a big box, wrapped in tissue paper, bound with string.

"This is from Pali and me," she said.

From the corner by the bookcase I drew out the gifts I had stashed there that morning. I handed them out, unwrapped. Milike took the gloves and held them a second, looking at them. Then she pulled one on and lifted her face, smiling.

"How pretty, Zoli. See–they fit! Thank you."

I felt momentarily that there was something wrong, but she put the other glove on and held her hands up to Pali. He nodded. I gave him his present in folded brown paper. He undid the paper and out fell the leather bookmark.

"Ah," he said, holding it up, "Zoli, will you show me how to use this?"

Milike laughed, but loudly, unlike her little-bell laugh.

"I'm sure you can figure it out," I said.

"Sit down, Zoli," Milike said. "Open yours from us. Come on."

I sat and pulled the string off the box. The tissue gave way easily. I lifted the lid, and caught my breath.

"Oh, I–I can't–this is more than I–"

"No," said Pali, "it is little enough for all you have done. For me alone."

"For all of us," said Milike. Her eyes shone at me. "Try them on." Her hands flitted like sparrows, carrying away the string and paper.

I looked up at their father, and he tipped his head at me, as if to say he agreed.

I picked up one shining black riding boot and worked it on as I had seen Pali do. I wiggled my heel through the tightness of the ankle and then my heel hit the sole with a satisfying thud. I stood up and bent my knee. The stiff leather creased across my ankle. I wanted more than anything right then to saddle a horse.

It was the day after that Milike and I went riding. We rode fast, and not far, the clouds gathering into a snow. The cold air turned her cheeks and nose a deep pink and flicked her hair out from under her woven scarf. I thought nothing could ever be as pretty as this woman riding a horse in the snow.

We came back to the stables in the lowering light and heavy air of a coming storm. The horses snorted frost as we unharnessed them, their stamping and blowing sounding hollow in the open walkway. I put up the saddles and led the horses around under their blankets a while. Milike watched me; I could feel her eyes following me.

She came then and took one horse, and we walked them in.

"You look good in those boots," she said.

I looked at the creases they were working into. I liked the feel of the boots, their snug, stiff leather bracing my legs.

"Thanks."

The gate slapped shut behind me. I felt again as I had when I had first held the gloves out to her.

"I'm sorry I couldn't get you something more than gloves," I said.

"Zoli, they're beautiful gloves. Don't you say any more about it now." She hung up the bridle, looping the reins lightly over the peg. She came around to me and took my arm.

Outside the snow had begun to fall.

1937

Professor Fenyo stalked the aisle again, prowling after answers. We hid among our books like so many rabbits in the brush.

"Still on holiday, are we?" he said. "Who is the longest reigning monarch in European history?"

At last, Hevesi said, "Franz Joseph, the First."

"Good. And how long was he king of Hungary?"

"Sixty-five years."

"Sixty-eight."

I knew about Franz Joseph. I just did not know that no other European had reigned so long.

"When was he king? Mr. Galambos."

"Of Austria, 1848 to 1916. Of Hungary, from 1867."

"And what should we know about his wife?"

I said, "Elizabeth was Austrian, but much loved by Hungarians because she learned to speak Magyar and spoke only that until she died."

"And how did she die?"

"She was assassinated," Hevesi said, "by an Italian anarchist."

Fenyo looked from one of us to the other.

"She was very beautiful," I said.

Fenyo smiled his little smile. "So she was."

I remembered her picture in the book, and when Fenyo went on to other topics, I quietly leafed to it. What drew me, I think, was the steady gaze she had, like Árpád's. I wished that I had been born sooner, in the days of kings. The present time seemed not to have any prospects for statues in it.

Hevesi did not leave as quickly as usual. I met him at the door.

"How are you?" I said.

"Fine." He pushed past me into the hall.

"Wait."

He stopped but did not look back. "What is it?"

"Can the past be the past? I mean, we should be allies here."

He drew a long breath. "The past is always the past. And that is the trouble, isn't it?"

"Look, you can't hold it against me about the scholarship at Komárom forever. I wish you had gotten it."

He faced me with a look that I sometimes saw in Pali, the hard look that comes with hard experience, with knowledge imposed rather than imparted.

"I do not hold it against you that you got the scholarship." His teeth barely opened to let the words through. "I hold it against the world that you got it because I am a Jew."

He took away my breath, my words, my wits. He spoke with an intensity that drove the words into me, and his eyes held me fixed.

"My father had to sell our horse–and pull the plow himself."

He walked away, and I stood in the doorway, weighted with a sudden guilt that was not mine. And I could not call after him that I would have given a thousand scholarships for a father who would do that for me.

*   *   *

There was a posted letter for me in the box, a rare happening. I pulled it out and went to sit on a bench outside to read it. The weather had become warm for April.

It was from Kovaly. I recognized his handwriting.

My dear Zoltán,

We certainly miss all you fellows here at Gymnásium. I keep expecting you all to be circled around the elm when I go home to lunch.

Do you have any Christian friends there? It's easy to lose your perspective among so many ideas about life as one finds at a university. I remember being quite lost sometimes and lonely. If you feel lonely, ever, please write me and let me know your mind. And stay in your Bible, son. Come up on the train when you are home, why don't you? Mrs. Kovaly and I would be glad to see you.

Another reason I'm writing is to tell you that Pastor Toth is building a boys' orphanage in Komárom. He feels strongly that the Lord wants him to do this. I knew you had worked with him and I thought you would be interested. I am going to help out as much as I can, until things are settled.

I read the rest of the letter, and then read the whole thing again. Somewhere I heard a girl laugh and fellows talking together. The trees were barely in bud, but the old sad feeling of spring came on me.

I sat there with the letter half-refolded in my hand until nearly dark, until only I was left, until Pali came looking for me.

"What is it?" he said.

"Ah, Pali. It's late, isn't it?"

"Is something wrong? Something bad in the letter?"

I looked down at the letter. "No. Nothing bad." ·

I could not define the feeling that Kovaly's words had given me. It was a longing without a clear object, or perhaps a sorrow without the heaviness.

"Come on, then," he said. "Let's walk down to Milike's and see what she has to eat."

Milike had chocolates still left from Christmas.

"I would have thought you had these all eaten up," Pali said.

"I had them hid," said Milike. She made tea and poured it into fragile cups with handles like question marks.

When she handed me my cup, she looked from it up to me and smiled, as though it were some special gift.

"These were Mama's," she said. "From Dresden."

"Thank you," I said.

I took the cup with its saucer as I might an injured bird and cradled it in my hands. Pali took his and balanced it on his knee with one hand. The radio played a kind of music that made me think of little children.

I ate a chocolate and sipped the tea until it cooled. The chocolates at Christmas had tasted somehow richer. It seemed as though taking them out of Budapest had weakened them a little.

I realized that Milike was looking at me, that she had asked me a question. A second later the question ran across my mind like an echo, only the last words coming to me over the distance—"home this summer."

I said, "I suppose so. I am expected."

Her smile dimmed only slightly and briefly, as when the smallest edge of a cloud passes by the sun. And then the smile was back, her head dipped at the chin and her eyes glancing up from under those lashes.

"You had better miss me then."

I felt the tips of my ears getting hot and my cheeks burning.

"But that's a long way off," she said. "And maybe Pali and I could come see you."

The color, I'm sure, drained out of my face as fast as it had come. The cup rattled as I put it in the saucer, and I had no answer.

Pali yawned. "Sorry. Too much study."

"I should hurry," I said. "I haven't written out my English paragraph."

"Teach me some more English, Zoli," Milike said. "Teach me how to ask for tea."

Some time later, I lay across my bed with an English-Hungarian dictionary and several sheets of crumpled paper. Red Hair appeared in the door.

"What are you doing?"

"Trying to write a paragraph in English."

"About what?"

"About anything."

He came into the room and hung over the foot rail of the bed. "Write about me."

I surveyed him. I knew the words for *red* and *hair*. I knew the words for *boy* and *school*. I picked up the dictionary.

"What are you looking up?"

"The word for *pest*."

He laughed. Red Hair, I had found, could not be insulted. He was wonderfully insulated by a sense of his own worth.

"I've been thinking," he said.

"Yes?"

"About those stories you used to read to us. Like David and Goliath."

I tried to frame a sentence about a boy with red hair, but I didn't know what verb was appropriate.

"And?"

"And I want to hear some more."

I wrote out the sentence, leaving a blank for the verb.

"What about your father? He doesn't want you hearing them, does he?"

"I won't tell him."

"Maybe Pali will read to you when he comes in."

"Why don't you?"

He stood up straight and grasped the rail with both hands. His eyes were wide and direct. His stare never wavered.

"Doesn't it help you anymore?"

I hesitated. I sat up and swung my feet around to the floor. I felt as though everything in the universe had ceased to move except for me. I thought I could hear drums.

"Listen, let me just tell you something, as a friend. Not as your hall supervisor, you understand?"

He nodded.

"I read the Bible because I believe God wants me to. I'm a Christian."

"What's that?"

I could still see the letter from Stelzer. I felt it like bars before my mind, as though I had to talk to this boy from a prison. I ran my hand over my face. It seemed to me that to answer this question would be to answer many questions that had hounded me from a distance these months.

I thought about David. Was my Goliath so much bigger?

"A Christian," I said, "is someone who knows he's no good himself and looks to Christ to save him."

There was freedom in the room again. The boy still gazed at me.

"Want to sit down?" I said.

He leaned back from the rail and eyed me. Then he came around and sat on the end of the bed. I opened my book bag and pulled out the Bible.

Chapter Seven
Shadows of Choices

The examinations at the university could not be compared with the ones at the Gymnásium. It would be comparing trains with bicycles. I studied until I fell asleep, surrounded by books, holding a book, under the electric light. When the bell jarred me in the mornings, it was more a matter of excavation than of getting up.

"You look awful," said Pali. "Don't you sleep?"

He came in, already dressed, and pulled out the chair.

"I sleep too much. I should never lie on the bed to read."

Pali shook his head. "What are you after? You have the grades."

"Not good enough."

He swung his leg over the chair back and sat down, his hands resting on the back and his chin resting on his hands.

"Well, I'd be glad for them."

I collected my papers and shifted the covers enough to count as making the bed.

"I have to check the hall."

"I've got time."

I stopped at the door. "All right. What?"

Pali pulled an envelope out of his jacket pocket and threw it at me. I caught only a corner of it, and the flap opened, spilling bills out. I lunged to catch the falling money.

"What's this?"

"Why, Zoli, it's money. Surely it hasn't been that long."

I straightened up and put the money back into the envelope. I felt the stubble on my face and the stiffness of my left shoulder, probably from sleeping on a book.

"I'm a dangerous man to trifle with right now."

Pali said, "I'm out of debt, Zoli." He grinned. "I thought that would get a smile from you."

I took a long shower, letting the hot water beat the stiffness out of my shoulder. I put my face under the water and felt its streaming warmth wash the worries out of me. Now that Pali was out of debt, I could be comfortable; I could buy Milike presents, take her to restaurants. My work as supervisor paid my way in school, but barely. Now–I turned off the water–it would be better.

I arrived for the English examination early. My classmates straggled in, only partly combed, only partly ready many of them, and I was comforted.

The teacher came in without smiling and closed the door. He did so with such force that it seemed that the door might never open again. He laid out the tests, one by one, on our desks, walking in his usual unhurried way. At last he turned to us.

"Begin."

Part I called for a translation, English into Hungarian. I could read several of the words in the first lines immediately, and then they began to sound vaguely familiar. I read on. I put my hand to my chin, hardly daring to believe what I was reading. It was the English version of the first chapter of Genesis. I glanced up at the teacher, who sat stone-faced at the front.

I put my pencil to the paper. "At the first, God created the heavens and the earth." The translation, I was sure, was close to perfect. I wrote fast, as though if I hesitated, the test would change into some other form, something unfamiliar.

The second part asked for three paragraphs, in English, on current world events. Fenyo had filled our heads with news. I had only to find the proper English way of telling it.

"Hitler sends guns to Spain. He hopes Mussolini will send guns. Hitler plans to perhaps fight Austria."

I could not remember what the teacher had said about keeping the *to* with the verb. In Latin, it is not a question. It seemed that in English there was a rule about that construction. I decided to go on with the paragraph and come back if there was time.

Time ran out. The bell took me by surprise.

"Pencils down. Close the tests."

There was a stir and a shuffle. I felt I needed to stretch.

"Thank you," the instructor said. "Dismissed."

The history exam was one essay question that somehow encompassed the rulers of Hungary from Árpád to Horthy. I drove my pencil, and myself, for the hour and a half and gratefully rested both at the bell.

I walked out into the warm spring with more pleasure in the season than I had had in many years. I wandered back to the dormitory. I wished I had a horse; it was a good day to ride.

I could not bring myself to study chemistry. I lay crossways on the bed and slept at once.

* * *

"Grades are up," Pali said.

I felt a momentary surge, as though my heart had expanded and contracted like a balloon.

Pali held out a paper. "Look at this."

His card held only B's and C's. I smiled and put out my hand. Pali took it, hard, and yanked it up and down twice.

"Thanks to you, Zoli."

"No, not just me."

I pulled up my suspenders, and my courage, and went toward the door.

Pali took off his jacket and tossed it over the chair. "Will you let me take you and Milike to dinner before you leave? I mean, if you haven't got something going already."

"Sure," I said. "That would be fine."

There was a pang in the words "before you leave." Partly it was an ache to be going and partly it was an ache to be gone, as though a moment could be both light and shadow. I understood the shadow, to be away from the learning and from Milike. But I still could not comprehend, or even name, the pull I felt toward Komárom, the longing I had felt reading Kovaly's letter.

A young man rapped on the already open door.

"Are you Zoltán Galambos?"

"Yes."

"Mr. Stelzer wants to see you. He sent me to tell you."

"Now?"

"Yes."

I looked over at Pali and shrugged.

Stelzer's door was closed. No one was in the outer office; so I sat down. I could hear someone typing off to the right.

"Hello? Excuse me."

There was no answer. The typing stopped and then began again. Abruptly, Stelzer's door opened and he looked out. He glanced at the outer office and then saw me.

"You, Galambos–come in here."

I stood by a chair until he motioned for me to take it.

He had a small face, long and thin. The lines from his nose to the corners of his mouth were deep, as though pressed in by years of contained aggravation. He pulled a sheaf of papers toward himself.

"Did I or did I not inform you that you were not to compel the students in your charge to listen to your personal religious opinions?"

"Yes, sir."

"Then I find it hard to understand why you continue to do so."

"I haven't, sir. I only answer questions when they are asked."

"A neat distinction, young man. I have good reason to believe you have disregarded my instructions entirely."

I sat silent, unable to fight an enemy I could not see.

"Furthermore, I have a report that one young man in your charge keeps liquor in his room."

"No!" I lowered my voice. "No, sir. I'm sure that's not true."

"Have you read your Bible to any student since you received my instructions?"

The mantle clock on the bookshelves ticked loudly. It seemed to be ticking off the moments left to me.

"Yes."

He tapped a pencil on the desk, let his fingers slide down it, turned it over with a tap, and let his fingers slide down. He pursed his lips.

"I don't like your kind, Mr. Galambos."

He shifted in his chair, and it squeaked deep in its workings.

"If I could just explain—"

"I did not ask for explanations. There is nothing to explain. You have done what I specifically told you I did not want done. I've seen you religionists operate. I won't have it."

He leaned forward suddenly and pulled a bottle from a drawer.

"This was taken from a room under your supervision."

I felt my heart catch.

"You are out of a position. Do not expect to work for this university again."

I could not rise or speak.

He brushed the air with a little stroke toward the door.

"Good day."

I think I stood then. The doorknob was cold in my hand. The blind slapped against the door as it shut behind me.

I threw open Pali's door. He was not there. I strode to the dresser and ripped open the drawers. I pulled out his clothes by the handfuls. I emptied the first drawer and started on the second.

"Zoli! What's the matter?"

Pali stood in the doorway, in a towel, his hair dripping.

I whipped open the third drawer and threw out the shirts. There was a clank, and my hand closed around the narrow neck of a bottle.

"This!" I said. "This is the matter!" I shook the bottle in the air.

Pali's mouth hung open, and his eyes squinted up.

"I don't–I haven't had–Zoli, I didn't bring that in."

"I trusted you!" I heard myself screaming. "I gave you my money! I gave you my help! This is how you repay me?"

Pali was walking toward me, his hands out and palms up.

"Zoli, I swear I–"

I dashed the bottle to the floor in front of him. The glass shattered open, and the liquid gushed out. I shoved past him.

"Zoli–"

I slammed the door against his words. I slammed my door against him.

He pounded on my door and called me again and again, but I had snapped the lock and did not intend to open it.

* * *

The train whistle screeched into the morning. I nudged my satchel along with my foot and carried two suitcases and all my books. The platform boards were uneven, and the drooping satchel caught on them. The third time, I gave the bag a walloping kick. It sprang upward and fell with a thud several paces away.

An old woman jumped and glared at me. Again the whistle screamed. I managed to get myself and the baggage into the car and find an empty seat. I slumped down and set my jaw, daring anyone to sit with me.

The train lurched out of the station. I glanced out the window as the building passed out of sight. Then I turned back and closed my eyes, for I did not want to see Bratislava disappear.

I could still see Milike, looking from me to Pali and back to me, frightened, sad, helpless. I pitied her, but I would not be swayed.

"Apologize," she had said to Pali.

"I have nothing to apologize for," he said.

She looked back to me, pleading.

I rubbed my eyes, and her face was lost in splotches behind my eyelids. The train rumbled and vibrated in a monotony that lulled me finally into an uncomfortable sleep.

Some time later I roused to hunger. I pulled a chunk of bread from the loaf I had stuck in my pocket. It was dry, but I did not care. The conductor came, took my ticket, and smiled.

"A ways yet, son," he said.

I nodded. I did not care about that either. I stuffed the bread into my mouth and chewed with vengeance. Later I tried to read a book, but after I had read the same page three times, I leaned my head against the window and dozed.

I heard Milike calling me, but it was raining so hard that I couldn't tell where her voice was coming from. I answered her and answered her. Then her face appeared in a high window lit with candles and hung with drapes. She waved for me to come inside, but I couldn't find the door. Every side of the building was the same, and the mud kept sucking at my feet.

"Nagy Megyer!"

The conductor's voice startled me awake. He called out the name of the next station again. I shook my head to clear it. When the train stopped, I got out and walked a while up and down the platform. Then we went on, the numbing rhythm of the wheels taking me over again.

Past dark, I heard the man call out "Komárom!"

My heart was suddenly racing. I pulled myself to the edge of the seat and ran my hand through my hair. When the conductor came by, I reached out for his arm.

"If I get off here tonight, can I use the rest of the ticket to Szilas tomorrow?"

"Of course," he said.

I let him go and sank back in my seat. The train was slowing, the rhythm of the wheels winding down. I tried to see out the window, as though what I should do might be written in the night somewhere.

"Komárom!"

The lights of the station appeared. I pulled forward in the seat again. The train rolled to a halt. The platform and the windows with light streaming through and the open doors looked like home. I grabbed up my cases and bundles and clambered out of the car.

I stood on the platform, holding my bags and books, until the train pulled out again. The few people who had been at the station were gone as well, as though the dark had silently erased them.

How long I stood there after the train had gone I do not know. At last, the finality of my decision broke in on me, and I grouped my bags around me on a bench to wait for morning.

A long time later a bird whistled somewhere, and then another. The blackness shifted into a gray, the outlines of trees emerging from the night and merging into each other. The gray shifted into a lighter gray, but still there were no colors in the leaves or the sky.

Just after daybreak, a man came onto the platform, keys jingling at his side. He whistled as he came, and when he saw me, he waved.

"Train's not due for hours," he said.

"Yes," I said.

He shrugged and nodded and unlocked the door. "Want to come in?"

I stood up among my bags. "Actually, I was wondering if I could stow my stuff here a while."

He looked me over. I knew that my rumpled clothes and my stubble of a beard did not speak well for me. But the man broke into a grin.

"Why not?"

I walked the road to the Gymnasium, as I had done hundreds of mornings before. The weeds and the fences and the road were exactly the same, and yet it seemed that nothing was familiar. Every nodding spring flower stood out to me, every rut in the road.

I stopped within sight of the buildings. Classes were still in here. Boys hurried along the same paths, yelling at each other as we had, carrying the same sets of books, looking for the same spots of shade to sit in and pretend to study.

I moved forward, as though returning from not just one year in Bratislava, but maybe hundreds of years in another country altogether. I felt so much older than the boys I passed, and lonely.

When I saw the elm, I felt my heart rise, and I had to keep myself from speaking to the tree. I sat down under the wide branches, half in the shade, half in the early sun. I put my head back on the trunk. It felt good.

"Zoltán? Zoltán Galambos?"

I knew the voice. I came to my feet, a smile taking control of me.

"Yes, Professor, it's me, I'm afraid."

Kovaly's eyes took me in the way they had that day in Szilas when he came to see Victor. His hand came out to mine, and when I took it, he put his other hand on my shoulder and pounded me soundly.

"I thought my imagination was getting the best of me when I looked out here. What brings you here?"

"I–" For the first time I realized I did not know exactly what I had hoped to accomplish by coming back to the Gymnásium, to the elm, to Kovaly.

"I was on my way to Szilas, and I–I just decided to get off here–a little while."

"Wonderful, my boy," said Kovaly. "I have Latin class now, you may remember, but can you stay until after that?"

I nodded. "Yes."

"Stay then." He put his finger out at me and shook it, as he might at a child. "I need to talk to you." He clapped my shoulder again and went in an old man's hurry into class. He had, I thought I noticed, a bit of a limp.

I sat down again. Now that I was here, I began to feel foolish. I almost wished that I had not agreed to stay. I put my arms on my knees and tried to pray, but the words got lost in my head.

Soon, too soon, Kovaly was coming back up the little slope to the elm.

"How have you been?" he said. He puffed as he came to the elm.

"Well," I said.

"Shall we walk?" he said. "I don't think I should ask these bones of mine to sit on the ground."

We passed from under the branches of the elm into the sunlight.

"I just thought I would stop and say hello," I said.

"I'm glad you did. Tell me about Bratislava."

His face was bright with interest. He kept his eyes mostly on me, glancing to where he was going from time to time.

"They have electric lights and electric bells in the dormitories."

He laughed. "And motorcars in the streets, I suppose."

"Not so many. Not like Budapest."

"Budapest? So you've been traveling."

I felt the conversation getting away from me.

"Just there, to Budapest."

"Ah. It's a lovely old city. I should like to see it again myself."

We walked past the administration building, and I had a momentary vision of Hevesi and myself as little ragged boys in the master's office. I looked down at my dusty shoes and wrinkled shirt. I ran my hands through my hair.

"Zoltán, what is it? You're not happy."

I felt the question like a needle in my heart, a thin, insistent pain. I did not know how to begin to answer him.

"What's happened, son?"

My eyes stung, and I hated myself for it.

"A lot."

We had stopped walking. Kovaly still looked at me, but he asked no more questions. For several moments I had no words, nor any breath to speak them had I had them.

"You remember Pali? The fellow I tutored my first year here. You introduced–"

"Yes, Pali! I've often prayed for him. Have you seen him?"

"He's in school at Bratislava."

Kovaly's eyebrows lifted in surprise and curiosity.

"Say on, Zoltán."

I told him about the fight on the lawn my first night at Bratislava, about Pali's drinking, about his new life. I told him about getting the supervisor's job, about tutoring Pali, about getting B's and C's, about meeting Milike, about Christmas and the riding boots and the gloves. When I got to the events of the last two days, I realized we had been walking again and were far out on the grounds.

"Then just when everything was smoothing out," I said, "my whole life is ruined by a bottle of vodka."

I flung the words out, as though they were evidence in court. I expected Kovaly to tell me about scholarships and faith and other jobs. I thought he might say something about Pali's behavior. But he did not. He said nothing for a long while.

He leaned against a fence and ran his hand across his cheek.

"Son, I've always admired your courage," he said. "And I have always been proud of you. You know that."

I looked down, without responding.

"And I've heard you say a hundred times that you were going to be a doctor. But, Zoltán, I've never once heard you say that God wants you to be a doctor."

I jerked my head up and looked him in the eye.

"What are you saying?"

"I'm only wondering whose goals have been thwarted here."

My jaw muscles tightened. "What's wrong with wanting to be a doctor?"

"Nothing, nothing at all. Don't be angry with me. All I ask is that you try to see the things that have happened from another angle. Perhaps God is trying to direct your steps to something else."

I stared at him as though I had never seen him before. "You think I should give up?"

He shook his head. "You misunderstand me," he said.

"I don't see how," I said.

"Zoltán, it's good to have goals. But we have to be sure they are the Lord's–"

"I should just roll over and quit?"

"Zoltán." His voice was hard; his eyes direct.

I looked down again.

"Hear me, now," he said. "If you tell me that you are sure that being a doctor is the Lord's will for you, I'll do everything I can to help you. But tell me, straight out."

I felt I might rip the boards from the fence and throw them.

"Is it?" he said.

"I don't know!"

He waited in silence a long time. I had my hands on the top of the fence, my knuckles white and the veins in my wrists bulging.

"Go over any obstacle to do God's will, Zoltán. But stop at the first one, if you're not sure."

I felt a sob squeezing up in me. I was betrayed on every hand.

"I have to be a doctor."

"Why?"

"I have to."

"Why?"

I wheeled around on him. "I won't be a farmer. I won't be poor and trapped and looked down on for the rest of my life!"

Kovaly did not move. His eyes welled with tears, and I scorned his weakness.

He said, "We can't see what shadows our choices will cast–but God can. He has to choose."

"I have to be going," I said. "I'm sorry I took up your time."

"No," he said, calmly, evenly, "you're sorry I didn't tell you what you wanted to hear."

I hated his sudden change toward me.

"I trusted you."

"Trust the Lord, Zoltán."

"You can say that easily enough. You can tell me to give up everything I ever wanted. You have everything. You do not know what I would be losing."

"You don't know what you would be gaining."

His eyes still watered, and his white hair shone.

"You have to get past your pride to see it," he said.

I felt a rush over me like cold water. I stood before him, unable to retaliate or even run.

"You are proud, son. Don't let it blind you."

"Blind me? I'm not the one who's blind, Professor. I can see well enough that for some reason you want me to give up my only chance for a real life. I thought you wanted me to go to school.''

''I do–if it's the right thing. Please just think–''

''The train will be leaving. I have to be on it.''

He only nodded.

I looked past him to the morning sun and squinted.

''Good-bye,'' I said.

He nodded again.

I walked away from him. I wanted to run, but I held myself back.

''If you need me, I'm here.''

His voice was clear and deep, like the countless times in the past, like the time I heard him praying for me in his house.

I hesitated and looked back. His cheeks were wet, but he smiled at me. I suddenly saw him in my mind, holding out shoe polish to me, a glass of water, a Bible.

There came a sudden weight against my chest, like a hand pressing down on my ribs. He looked like winter in the new greenness of the meadow, with his dark gray suit and his white hair. His shadow reached nearly to my feet. For a moment, I had a clear vision of myself had this man's shadow never come over me.

The sob I had held down came out with my words.

''Oh, sir, I'm sorry. I'm so sorry.''

Kovaly took a step toward me. I shook my head.

''I have to go. I'm sorry.''

I ran that time, before he could speak.

Chapter Eight
Orphans

My father's house was obscured by the cherry blossoms coming on my grandfather's trees. A thin stream of smoke came winding out from the chimney. I wondered whether anyone was looking for me.

I walked the lane past the barn, and the smell of cows and horses wafted to me. It was not an unpleasant smell, not nearly as repugnant as I seemed to have remembered. The lane was not muddy as it sometimes was in the spring.

The talk with Kovaly weighed upon me more than the bags I carried. I felt as though I had run a long way, as though my lungs ached from the effort of pulling in enough air.

I stopped briefly before going into the house and listened. I could hear someone working in the kitchen, but no talking. I set down my things quietly and flexed my arms, stiff with the strain of carrying all that from the station. I opened the door and went in. My mother was putting a stick of wood in the stove.

"Hello, Mama."

"Zoltán!" She shoved the wood in and wiped her hands on her apron. "You should have written that you were coming."

She crossed the kitchen and embraced me quickly. It surprised me so that I drew in a breath. She stepped back from me.

"How long are you here?"

"I don't know," I said. "For the summer, at least."

"Dezső!" she called. "Dezső, come here. Zoltán's home!"

There was the scrape of a chair and then padding footsteps. A much grown Dezső swung open the door.

"Dr. Zoli!"

A pain ran down my arms and out my fingers at the title.

"Hello, Dezső."

My mother laughed.

"Here is some money. Run get us some pastries from the bakery."

Dezső went out like an arrow from a bow.

"And don't eat any on the way," she called after him.

"Where's Papa?"

"He and Victor are plowing." She nodded toward the field.

I could not catch from her gesture or tone what I might expect from them as a reception.

"Béla's getting the cows. Bring in your things," she said. "You know where to go, I expect?"

"What about Victor? Isn't that his room now?"

She shook her head. "He mostly sleeps in the barn anymore. Works 'til he can't stumble and then falls asleep out there."

Her tone was flat, as though she were telling me about one of the horses.

The door creaked in the same way, and the oil lamp sat in the same spot on the stand by the bed. I dropped the baggage and went to the window. Papa walked behind one horse, stooped a little, as though he plowed for the whole world. I could not see Victor anywhere.

The barn was also unchanged, except for one large detail. A machine, a thresher, took up a great portion of the barn floor. I walked around the thing, bending down to look into it, straining up to see over it. Dark patches on the floor told me oil had leaked from it not long ago.

It was dusty and rusted here and there. I pulled a chain, and gears moved with a squeal somewhere deep in it. My hand came away black with grease.

Far off I heard the clanking of cowbells and a boy's voice, high and insistent. I swung down the ladder to the stanchions. Over the rise behind the barn, Béla came with a switch, flailing the heels of the cows.

The cows bawled. When Béla came into the barn, he spied me. He stopped short and regarded me as he might a stranger who had wandered in.

"Hello, Béla," I said.

"Hello."

"Good to see you."

He nodded. He went down the line, tying the cows to their posts.

"You're a lot taller in a year," I said.

He straightened up, at the far end of the barn, and looked back at me.

"Did you see the thresher Victor bought?"

"Victor? How did he–"

"Working around, extra. Saving up from crops last fall. He's going to fix it, and then we can really make some money."

I felt tired, as though I had walked from Bratislava.

"Good," I said.

When Papa and Victor came down from the fields, I had the milking nearly done. Papa stood at the door; I could feel him looking in at me.

"Can milk still?" he said.

"I can," I said.

I glanced up at his silhouette in the doorway. He held his hands on his hips, and his arms made diamonds with his body, lit from behind. But I felt that he was not displeased to see me.

Victor stood behind Papa slightly and glared at me. I nodded to him, and he walked away, leading the horses. I turned back to my milking.

There was more talk at supper than I remembered ever having heard in a week's time in that house before.

"What do they say, in Bratislava, about this Hitler?" My father had not given up his newspapers, apparently.

I swallowed my food half-chewed to answer quickly.

"That he is gaining allies, perhaps to try Austria again."

Papa nodded. "Mussolini."

"Yes. And Spain, if it falls."

Victor speared his sausage as though it were still able to run from him.

When my father said no more, I turned to Victor.

"That's quite a feat, to buy a thresher."

His cheeks reddened, but I knew the comment set well with him.

"Not so much," he said.

"It took months of extra work," Béla said. "Night and day."

Béla's eyes gleamed as he spoke. He looked to Victor, but Victor only bit off a piece of bread.

"Does it need much fixing?" I said.

"No."

"Can I help with it?"

He looked over at me as though I had offered to shoot him.

"I don't need any help."

"Tell us about school," said Mama.

* * *

The apple trees blossomed, and faded into leaf, and put out hard green marbles that always by some miracle became apples. We planted the fields, Victor, Papa, Béla, and I, in the same old way, until we were too tired to eat, and then dragged ourselves up the next morning to go at it again.

At last the seeds were in the ground, and it rained, a steady, warm rain, for a day and a night. We agreed, without any words or any discernible sign, that a little rest could be had.

I took a book on Hungarian history to the loft of the barn and made a seat in the old hay by the back wall. Enough light came in through the holes and cracks to serve.

Béla climbed up the ladder toward noon, his head suddenly appearing at the end of the loft, and then his hand, and then the rest of him.

"What's that?" I said.

"The mail," he said.

The return address was the University in Bratislava. I peeled open the envelope and braced myself.

No scholarships were awarded, it said, to anyone with less than a B+ average. It said this politely, apologetically, and firmly.

I put the letter back into the envelope and nodded to myself.

"And this," said Béla. He pulled another, smaller envelope from his belt behind him and drew it slowly under his nose.

"It smells good," he said.

"Give me that."

It did smell vaguely of Milike's perfume.

"Who's it from?" Béla said.

"A friend in Bratislava, is all."

Béla sat down next to me and waited for me to open the letter.

"What are you doing?"

"Well, if it's just a friend, I didn't think you'd mind my reading it."

"Well, I do."

Béla snorted, just the way Victor always did, and pushed himself up.

"That's what I thought," he said.

I held the letter for several minutes before I unsealed it. I felt the smooth paper and thought that Milike had only days before held it in her hand.

My dearest Zoli,

It's like you have been gone forever. And it's not even a month yet. If we had parted better, I think I could stand it more.

Pali and I have talked and talked. He says he had nothing to do with what happened and I believe him. Really I do, Zoli. I know my brother—I wish you could believe me, if not him.

Papa knows nothing of the trouble, of course, and keeps asking when "my young doctor" is coming for another visit. Do you think you could, Zoli? I miss you so.

Or could I come there? I could stay in a hotel nearby or something, if you don't have room in your house. We have to talk. This long silence isn't possible for me any more. Please let me hear from you.

I leaned my head back against the rough boards and closed my eyes.

"I miss you, too," I said.

Milike was too easily led. How did she think that the bottle had gotten in Pali's dresser anyway? The entire memory was clouded over as though I had to look at it through a red haze.

I opened my eyes and saw the old hay around me, an appropriate sight for one whose future looked as mine did: worn out, dull, colorless. I pulled a piece of hay up and stuck it between my lips and chewed on it. It had a moldy taste.

I closed the book and jerked myself up from the hay and the contemplation. What more was there to think about? I could not get enough money for another year of school, and I could not keep my grades high enough if I worked more during the semester.

I swung my leg over the rail and found the ladder with my foot.

"All right," I said, "what is it You want me to do?"

"What?"

I stopped on the ladder and looked behind me and down. Victor stood on the barn floor just inside the door. I wiped my face across my sleeve and hung there on the ladder, suspended between resolve and challenge.

"Nothing," I said. "I wasn't talking to you."

Victor sneered. "Talking to God again?"

I came on down the ladder.

"Yes," I said. "I was."

Victor picked up his wooden box of tools and shoved it toward the thresher. He slid himself under the machine and dragged the box toward him.

"Religion is for cripples," he said.

"Who is not crippled?" I asked.

Victor rolled out slightly and looked at me directly, intently, for the first time in years.

"Me," he said. "You don't see me whining to God, do you?"

"Nobody can stand alone forever, Victor."

"Not forever maybe," he said, "but long enough."

He ducked back to his machine and worked the wrench with energy. I watched him, my heart surging, more with anger or pity I could not tell.

*   *   *

The school that had been overwhelming when I was a child seemed small now and tattered. The floorboards were worn, and the bench in the back, where I had sat waiting for Victor to take his tests, was marred by rings where the water bucket had sat.

I walked the aisle and took the teacher's place at the front. Perhaps, I thought, I could be a teacher. I had sufficient education for this village, surely.

I looked down on the front row, where I had sat that first year, fifteen years before, where my teacher coming in, and finding me early again, brought me his songbook, *Zsoltáros Könyv*. To the right was the cupboard, the closed shelves of books, that the teacher kept his treasures in.

For a moment I held back, a student, a child under the laws of my youth, under the invisible restraints of rules still binding but not enforceable. The wooden handle turned easily, as though it no longer had the right or need to keep me out. And there was the songbook, with the gold letters, and the well-turned pages.

Many of the songs I remembered from those days, and many I had seen since, in my Bible, some underlined, some put to memory. I found the first one I had learned.

God be merciful unto us, and bless us;
God cause his face to shine upon us.

I remembered how I had not liked the tune. And had I not asked about another then? I turned the page over, and it came to me what my teacher had said–"This is for a sadder heart than yours." Perhaps now he would think I had lived enough to read it.

Save me, O God; for the waters flood my soul.
There is no standing where these waters roll.
They that hate me wrongly wait to take me;
O my God, do thou hear and not forsake me.

The words were like medicine to me, like comfort for a long sorrow. I read the song again, but I could not sing it.

That night in the low light of the lamp, I found the Psalm and read it.

Save me, O God; for the waters are come in unto my soul.

It seemed I could feel the cold darkness of those waters David had sung of even then at my feet.

> *O God, thou knowest my foolishness; and my sins are not hid from thee.*
>
> *Let not them that wait on thee, O Lord God of hosts, be ashamed for my sake: let not those that seek thee be confounded for my sake, O God of Israel.*
>
> *Because for thy sake I have borne reproach; shame hath covered my face.*
>
> *I am a stranger unto my brethern, and an alien unto my mother's children.*

My eyes stung; old wounds, never quite healed, harrowed me with familiar pain.

> *Hear me, O Lord; for thy lovingkindness is good: turn unto me according to the multitude of thy tender mercies.*
>
> *And hide not thy face from thy servant; for I am in trouble: hear me speedily.*
>
> *Draw nigh unto my soul, and redeem it: deliver me because of mine enemies.*
>
> *Thou hast known my reproach, and my shame, and my dishonor: mine adversaries are all before thee.*

A day ago I would have read this Psalm with vengeance; but now I felt only that I wanted to hide under the shadow of my God, to wait in peace for His unfolding.

> *Let their table become a snare before them: and that which should have been for their welfare, let it become a trap.*

The anger all ran out of me, and I felt sleep coming over me.

> *But I am poor and sorrowful: let thy salvation, O God, set me up on high.*

It was true, as the teacher had known, that there would be a day when I was ready to read this Psalm, when my experience would fit me for it. I felt myself a child again, but before the great Teacher now.

I turned down the lamp and lay back. Instead of the long, anguished prayers of the many nights before, I said only, aloud in the darkness, "I surrender," and slept.

* * *

In the following days, I memorized that Psalm, and wrote a short and much overdue letter to Professor Kovaly. I went about my work with the sudden lightness of having laid down a weight carried too long.

"Zoltán."

Papa's voice came from the other end of the barn floor.

"Yes?"

"Lend a hand."

He had thrown the harness over the horses and left it for me to fasten.

I adjusted the collars and straightened the lines out. I reached under for the belly strap, talking to the horses quietly.

Papa said, "Béla says you have a girl."

I pulled the strap up to the buckle on the trace and tried to think whether I had heard him right. I threaded the underside strap behind the trace and latched it to the breeching.

"I know a girl in Bratislava. A sister of–"

I ran my hand along the trace.

"An old friend," I finished.

"Rich?"

"Her father is, somewhat."

He laid the whiffletrees on the floor and did not speak for so long that I thought the lengthiest conversation I had ever had with my father was over. He hooked the traces to the trees with the swiftness borne of years of repeated work.

I led the horses around to the door, glancing at him when I did, to see that he had picked up the whiffletrees and was following and also to see what I could read in his face.

We hitched the horses to the doubletree on the cultivator.

"Well," he said, "be at least as rich as that."

He came around to take the lines. His face seemed as worn as the gray boards on the barn. He stooped more and more, as though he had the whole fifty acres on his shoulders, as though he were a man run by a farm rather than a man running a farm. His eyes, though, had the look of someone worn down by more than work.

"I'll do this," I said.

I kept the lines in my hands and dipped my head to him.

He looked at me, and though he did not smile, his eyes seemed to brighten just a second, as when a wick is turned up ever so slightly in the lamp. He stepped back and had begun to turn away.

"Papa."

He stopped and looked at me vaguely, through me and beyond me, more than at me.

I looked down and then up to him again.

"Thank you."

His lip curled a little under his mustache.

"What for?"

"For teaching me to learn by watching," I said.

He regarded me silently for a moment and then went away into the barn.

I blinked–the sun coming directly over the horizon at me–and clicked to the horses. The cultivator rattled over the rough ground, and I came behind in its dust.

My hands were raw by the end of the day from the lines running through my fingers. The horses were dark with sweat under the straps of their harness, and they were snorting the dust from their noses.

I felt my face caked with the dried mud of my own sweat and the flying dust. I turned the horses toward the barn, and they went with new energy down the slope. The smell of the turned earth and the new plants was sweet, and the jingle of the harness sounded like little bells.

I unharnessed the team and walked them, to cool them and to shake from myself the labors of the day. From the far side of the barn I could see the cherry trees drooping with fruit, and I wondered whether Dezső and Béla had been after it.

In the house the scent of custard pie hung in the air. My mouth watered just to smell the nutmeg.

Mama looked up and smiled when I came in, but she said nothing. Her hair was pulled up neatly, and her apron was fresh. For a moment, I felt I had been in that same spot before, watching my mother get a pie from the oven. It seemed to be an older memory than even the white horse. It hovered in my mind only a second, and then was gone like a little puff of smoke. Later I doubted it altogether, for the warmth of the emotion it stirred was as foreign to me as the stars.

* * *

Béla came from the cherry trees with a pan of cherries, eating them as he walked and grinning at me.

"Béla–"

He waved his hand back and forth at me and chewed enormously, tipping back his head to keep the juice from running out.

"Don't worry," he said, through the mouthful, "nobody cares."

I drew in a breath, intending to send it out laden with advice, but Béla spoke first.

"Grandfather died four months ago. Didn't anyone tell you?"

He wiped his mouth on his arm. "Papa's getting the farm."

He might have told me the barn had burned down behind me and created no more astonishment in me.

"When?"

Béla shrugged. He carried the pan into the house. I gazed across the way at the house and land that had been a foreign country to me all those years. The man who had fathered my father was dead, and I felt not the least pain.

I began to see my mother's light spirits through a clearer window now. And my father's comment—"be at least as rich as that"—had a root to spring from. Their happiness squeezed in on me from all directions, and more than any sadness had, this awareness made me sick at heart.

The day after a thunderstorm, I got the letter. From the envelope I could not have told it was any more significant than any other, for the stamp was slightly crooked and the hand a bit unsteady. Nor could I have told by the sender what a document in my small history it would be. Kovaly would reply; I knew that.

I opened it as I walked. And then I slowed, and stopped. The breeze lifted the corners of the paper, as though the words were not weighty, as though the message were not the anchor to hold me to my decision.

I folded the letter carefully again and put it in the envelope. The rain had washed everything; the sun glistened from every leaf and blade. I took a longer stride when I walked again.

The meal that evening was as pleasant a time as I could ever remember in that house. Victor, although mostly silent, was not belligerent. My mother spoke to my father without any undercurrent of resentment, though her conversation was about trivial happenings in the village. The momentary calm nearly swept me in, nearly made me believe that all was at last well.

Béla said, "Papa, when will you get Grandfather's farm?"

Papa shook his head.

"Hush, Béla," said Mama.

"I want to know," he said.

My mother glanced at my father, and there it was again, that old accusation, the look of someone betrayed.

"It takes time," Papa said.

The statement quieted the talk, but not the looks, not completely.

I felt the letter in my pocket, and my heart pounded in my throat.

"I–"

Mama looked to me and so did Dezső. When I did not continue, Papa and my other brothers brought their eyes up.

"I got some news today," I said.

They waited.

"And I've made a decision. I am needed in Komárom. To run a new orphanage there."

No one spoke or moved.

"What?" My mother's voice was hardly a breath.

"I don't think I am to go to school anymore–right now," I said.

I could hear the words as they must have heard them, strange and errant, unconnected. I dared not look at Mama.

"What kind of work is that?" Papa said. His voice had the edge that had cut into me as a child.

"It's what I must do," I said. "I know it is."

My mother stood slowly, as though it might be the last time she would ever get up from her chair.

"That is a nobody's job," she said. She spoke so quietly that the ticking of a clock might have kept me from hearing her.

"Mama, I want–"

"I do not hear you," she said, "you who might have saved us all."

She left the table and went into her room. The door clicked shut. Papa sat still, leaning on the table, his eyes fixed ahead. Béla and Dezső gazed at me. Victor folded his hands across his stomach and smiled.

The sun went down, and a shallow moon replaced it. A watery light spread over me from it, but still I sat on the low wall behind the house. I felt as though the Zoli who had grown up in this house were someone I had known only casually, like a distant cousin who, though related to me, was so different from me.

Late in the night, my mother appeared in the doorway of my room, a lamp in her hand, her hair down and not braided.

"Get out of this house," she said.

I sat up.

"Take only the clothes you wore from the train."

"Mama, please–"

"I do not know you," she said. "Do not call me your mother."

I thought perhaps she was walking in her sleep. I stepped toward her.

"Stop," she said. "Do not take anything from here. You own nothing. You are nothing. I do not want to see you again. Never come here, never write."

I heard her, but I could not take in the words.

She turned away, the lamp casting a wild glow around her head and shoulders, and passed beyond the threshold. I stood in the dark, debating whether this apparition had been real, had meant what it said.

The light of morning soon came, but it did not change anything that had passed in the night. My father sat silent in his chair. My mother did not come out of her room.

"Papa?"

He did not look at me, or stir, or speak. My throat was hot, and my eyes burned.

"Tell Mama I have only the clothes I bought for myself."

I looked again toward her door. Then I went out, past the fences and the yard, and down the lane. The sky was gray, but not threatening, and the air was cool.

The last thing I remember of that long walk was Victor's laugh echoing from the barn.

* * *

The train rumbled through the morning as it had hundreds of times before, carrying me to Komárom. I looked back at the station until it disappeared, until Szilas was no more than a direction I might point in and say, "My village is that way."

I sat down in the seat, beside my books. The rhythm of the tracks stilled me, comforted me. And then I thought again of all that had come before, and my heart seized up, as though some hand had squeezed it.

In a little while, I felt for the New Testament Kovaly had given me, its familiar weight in my pocket, its cover worn smooth at the edges. I pulled it out and drew back the flyleaf. On the white page Kovaly had written me a message years before. He had meant it then for a boy still looking for his way, but it served just as certainly now for a young man still coming to himself.

Zoltán,
I am praying for you—that you will understand what it is
to be a child of the King.

Kindly,
Henrik Kovaly

My breaths came easier, and I felt my veins relax, the blood running through them, through me, with courage and joy. I laid my head back on the seat and looked out on the meadows rolling by. I left in them every false regret.

"Komárom," the conductor said.

The word was warm, like a fine September day, bright and clear and full of reward. It came to me then, as a truth long known but only suddenly realized, that I was not leaving my home, but coming to it.